Escape to Macaya

Hall Franklin Duncan, Ph.D.

Copyright © 2014 Hall Franklin Duncan, Ph.D.

First Edition

PUBLISHED BY

Humor and Communication LLC
YOUNG ADULT LIBRARY

929 Jacobs Street, Edmond, OK 73034
P.O. Box 7104, Edmond, OK 73083

www.hallduncan.com   info@hallduncan.com

A slave child and his endangered pet dash for freedom in Haiti

JANUARY 2014

DYE MON, GEN MON
"Beyond the mountain is another mountain."
Haitian Creole Proverb

Escape
to Macaya

by
Hall Franklin Duncan, Ph.D.

ISBN-13: 978-1494929244
ISBN-10: 1494929244

Library of Congress Control Number: 2014900454

Printed in U.S.A.

This Book is Dedicated…

> To Daniel and Franklin,
> Forgive me when I didn't hear
> your cry for help in Africa.
>
> and…
>
> To Children in Slavery in Haiti
> and around the world.
> I hear your cries every day.

Illustrations by the author

Thanks to
My Many Talented Friends

Merci
Beaucoup!

Editors

Ken Bever	Stephanie Driver
Dr. Ron & Doris Bever	Dr. Bruce Duncan
Rev. Jim & Lou Ann Jones	Sandy Hockenbury

Hope for Haiti's Children, and Reverend Jim Jones, United Methodist Conference School of Missions on Haiti	Bibliography research, maps and on-site information;
Victor Driver, Sr.	Book design, production and typography
Margaret Gaeddert	Cover art
Leslie and Tod Hardin	Review
Bob Myers	Aerial Photography Research
OKC Kid Writers Society Oklahoma City Chapter of Children's Book Writers and Illustrators	Story plot and character review
Earlene Smith	Typography

Escape to Macaya

Contents

Meet
the Author

Hall Franklin Duncan, Ph.D.

**"Dr. D", Writer/Illustrator, Bases Children's Books
on Life Experiences!**

Dr. Duncan was born and raised in Oklahoma City.

He is a retired professor of advertising design and illustration from the University of Central Oklahoma. His students call him "Dr. D."

He received the Governor of Oklahoma's "Special Recognition Arts Award" in 2008 for his children's books and school reading programs.

He was educated in China, Europe, South Africa and the United States working his way home on a freighter from Antwerp to Houston. Dr. Duncan served for thirteen years as a Christian missionary to Africa in literacy and book illustration. He trained artists in eleven countries.

Dr. Duncan is one of the few illustrators in the world to hold a Ph.D. in the study of pictorial perception habits of children. This work resulted in his writing over ten books and three cartoon features for young readers.

His research has been published by New Reader's Press, Syracuse, New York; Human Sciences Research Council, Witwatersrand University Press, Johannesburg, South Africa; and the University of Cambridge, UK.

His wife, Lois, died unexpectedly in 2011. She assisted Dr. Duncan in his international humor workshops. Dr. Duncan resides in his studio cottage in Edmond, Oklahoma.

Escape to Macaya

An Introduction

Haiti is extremely complicated. Constant changes are observed and analyzed through many perspectives.

The author does not present this novel as a complete truth about these magnificent people, though much is based on facts. The purpose of the story is to awaken people of all ages, wherever they are, to do what is right for humanity.

I have written the last two chapters as if they already have occurred. But in reality, they will take place during the next decade to include the remarkable effects of cell phone technology, improved transportation, and education development.

The author challenges all of his readers to dedicate their talents and wealth to eliminate the slavery that many children are brutally forced to endure. Haiti is a classic case. The author is also aware of this sickness in his own neighborhood in the United States.

In spite of the child slavery around them, many Haitians pursue lives of peace and laughter in the midst of disease, hunger and poverty.

Children are always our hope for a world of love, respect and care for others. Please act now!

Dr. Hall Duncan
January 2014

Escape to Macaya

Frequently Asked Questions

Escape to Macaya

Main Characters

ANDRÉ ARNAUD
Fourteen year old student at Sunshine Academy, Mount Macaya, Haiti. Father, Henri, School Maintenance Director. Mother, Annette, Manager Visitors' Cottage. One sister, Héléne.

"HOOT" THE HUTIA
Young Hispanolian hutia. Lives protected in Mount Macaya endangered animal sanctuary.

PAUL "LE TIGRE" NOIR
Notorious drugs, diamonds and armaments smuggler in Haiti. Dying from AIDS. Keeps rare white tiger pet.

MADAME NOIR
Wife of "Le Tigre" (Tiger) Noir. Cruel, heavy drinker, practices voodoo and Catholicism.

DOMINIQUE
Bodyguard for Le Tigre Noir. Twitching smile. Weighs 250 pounds. Keeps German Luger strapped to his body. Street name: "Dom".

COUTEAU
"Yes man" for Dominique. Pockmarked face, wiry, reddish kinky hair. Wears ripped jeans and frayed Yankee ball cap.
Street name: "The Knife."

Supporting Characters

JABOU
Madame Noir's brother. Police Captain in Port-au-Prince. Sells prison labor.
Street name: "Le Fouret" (the Whip).

BEATRICE NOIR
Madame Noir's teenage daughter.

MICHAEL NOIR
Madame Noir's teenage son.

THE FONTAINES
Marie and Pierre. Canadian scientists and Directors of Save Macaya Research Center.

MR. & MRS. THOMPSON
Missionary educators in charge of Sunshine Academy, Mount Macaya.

JEAN
Last restavec of Madame Noir.

VINCENT LAVALIER
Prosperous Haitian importer.

HENRI ARNAUD
Andre's father

Geographical Locations for the Story:
Western Haiti, Macaya Mountain and Port-au-Prince
The Year: Today

All characters appearing in this story are fictitious. Any resemblance to a real person, alive or dead, is coincidental.

Escape to Macaya

Chapters

Where is Haiti?

It is the western third of the tropical Caribbean Island of Hispaniola. Slightly larger than Vermont, it lies about 50 miles southeast of Cuba.

The original inhabitants, the Taino Indians, called it 'Hayti' (Land of the Mountains). The people today speak mainly Haitian Creole.

1

Trapped

A propane tank exploded, hurling 14-year old André across the road from his house.

He gasped for air. His lungs burned. He believed he was going to die.

He tried to sit up, but splintered logs pinned him down. His shredded T-shirt and shorts revealed painful burns, cuts and bruises over his body. Exhausted. Numb. Too weak to shout for help, he rolled his head away from the stench of rotting garbage and a dead dog.

André lived with his parents and little sister Hélène in a small village nestled on the northern slope of Mount Macaya in western Haiti. Its people had not experienced such a destructive fire since 10 years ago, when armed thugs from the south coast set the town ablaze.

The fire was a tragic accident. Hélène had tripped as she placed a kerosene lantern on a windowsill. The kerosene rapidly reached the charcoal fire where her mother had been frying bread to sell in tomorrow's market.

Hélène had screamed as her dress had caught fire and flames raced up the walls. The roof had collapsed, killing Helene and her mother instantly. The fire spread to the nearby propane filling station.

André recalled he was carrying charcoal and was racing toward the fire at his home. A sudden blast shot him across the road where he landed on top of a dump of rotting garbage. The soft landing saved his life.

André remembered saying good-bye to his father, Henri, who had left for Jeremie, a seaport town, a day's drive away. His dad promised to return with building supplies and food for the mission school, Sunshine Academy, where he worked as a handyman.

Blinded by a swirling mushroom of black smoke and hot ash, André could only wait to be rescued.

He heard a church bell clanging an alarm. A lost child screamed for his grandmother. Families fled into the mountains with only a few clothes and surviving goats.

Hours passed. Temperatures dropped. Everything became coldly silent. André lapsed in and out of consciousness.

Dawn's warming rays revived André. "It's daylight. I've got to be found." He thought.

His hopes were quickly shattered. He heard

pistol shots and the rat-a-tats of machine gun fire.

Shouts of looters echoed through the valley below. Neighbors fought strangers to protect anything that survived the fire. The village became a battleground. The nearest police station was two hours away and they rarely visited this community.

A blue truck screeched to a stop. André froze. Heavy footsteps crunched toward him. A cold rough hand brushed ashes from his forehead. He felt others lifting the debris off his chest. He breathed more easily.

A strange voice growled from a twisted smile, "What have we here?"

André shook and looked up. A huge black man towered above him. "Please don't hurt me," André begged.

Who is a Restavec?

A restavec is a Haitian child usu-ally between the ages of 4 and 18 sold by destitute parents to a family who promises to provide their child with food, shelter, clothing, medical care, and schooling in exchange for working in their home.

Unfortunately, most restavecs are treated as child slaves – severely neglected, starved, and abused as outcasts. Approximately 225,000 Haitian children are estimated to be restavecs by UNICEF.

The Haitian Creole term is derived from the French "rester avec" which means "to stay" or "remain with".

2

Tricked

"Who are you?" André gasped.

"I'm your friend," the stranger lisped. "Call me Dom. What does your mother call you?"

"A-A-A-André," he slurred. "I'm so-o-o tired. I'm sick. I hurt all over."

Dom gently raised André's head and lowered a plastic bottle of water. "Here, sip this."

André gulped, swallowing hard. Water dribbled down his T-shirt.

Dom yelled to his companion, Couteau. "Let's put this kid in the pickup. You take his legs."

"Easy! We need to stop his bleeding. These rags should do it." Dom cautioned.

Dom, a big ebony Haitian, swaggered his 250 pounds like a prizefighter.

Couteau sported a yellowish-tan complexion topped by kinky reddish-brown hair. He joked that his ancestors were Caribbean pirates. He was short and quick on his feet. A smallpox survivor, his face resembled rough pitted sandpaper.

André winced in pain as he lay stretched out on

the truck's tailgate. Offered fruit, he nibbled down a banana and orange. Feeling stronger, he thought maybe these guys weren't so bad after all.

"We're taking you to our home, André. You'll be more comfortable there with lots of good food and rest. We need to get medicine on those bruises and cuts."

Dom patted André's shoulder softly. "And we'll find your parents."

"You won't find my mother and sister." André sobbed. "Look! Our house is gone."

"Where is your father?" Couteau asked.

"In Jeremie."

"What's he doing there?"

"Getting stuff for the school." André replied.

"When's he coming back?"

"Tomorrow night."

"Good, we'll head that way. Hopefully we will find him." Dom promised.

André studied Dom's face carefully. Dom's twitching smile made him nervous. A scar ran across Dom's right cheek to his left upper lip, revealing two missing front teeth. Dom's breath stank of strong tobacco.

André wondered about the relationship between his "rescuers." He watched Dom scream and curse at Couteau.

He observed how Couteau avoided angering Dom with his constant "Sorry, boss."

Paul Robert, a school classmate, approached the truck.

"Are you okay, André?"

Dom replied, "He'll be fine. You run along."

Peering inside the pickup, Paul Robert screamed, "André, that's my mom's sewing machine and my dad's radio in their truck. They're robbers! Run, André, run!"

André recognized more items from Paul Robert's home, including a metal chest with baby Jesus on the lid and a big red bowl.

André dropped quickly to the ground and took two steps. Clubbed by a blow to the back of his head, he collapsed face down in the mud. His head was racked with pain.

Dom shouted, "Clean his mouth out. Tie his hands and legs." He tossed a sugar sack to Couteau. "Here, cover his head. Make sure he can breathe. He must arrive in Port-au-Prince alive."

"If he screams, I'll gag him." Couteau replied.

Dom jumped into the pickup, switched on the ignition and floor-boarded the gas pedal.

"We've got to get out of here now!" he yelled.

Hearing the commotion, Paul Robert's grandfather came running to see what was happening.

Dom cursed the grandfather, who stood whacking the windshield with his cane and blocking the pickup with Paul Robert at his side.

Dom stiffened his neck, lowered his head, and drove directly into them. Paul Robert tackled his grandfather, and rolled him away from certain death.

"We should have shot them!" Couteau snarled. "And look, that old geezer cracked your windshield!"

Dom nursed the pickup around the ruts lashed into the road by recent hurricane rains.

André lay tightly roped behind the pickup's cab, his head bleeding and swelling. An hour passed. Dom called Tigre Noir on his cell phone. He shouted above the noise of the whirring engine. André could hear his menacing voice.

"Our trip's going well, boss. We got the animal and lots of good selling loot. And listen carefully, tell Madame Noir, we've got her a restavec, a nice healthy one to replace the one killed at the police station.

"I'll call you tomorrow from Les Cayes. Bye." He clicked off.

All this sounded strangely evil to André.

A rolled wad of stolen clothing cushioned André as he lay in the bed of the pickup.

He prayed for survival. He had never felt so alone before. He was living now in another world dominated by grown-ups who robbed and hurt those suffering around them.

He thanked God for his dad and for his schoolmates and teachers who would be frantically searching for him. He knew they would not give up until they found him. His biggest weapon to end this nightmare was hope and his faith in a God of love. He remembered the horrors Jesus faced. The rejection. The beatings. And all by fellow neighbors whom Jesus loved and served.

The pickup passed women hawking cooked food. André couldn't see them, but the smell triggered his hunger. He thought about the pre-school orphans at Sunshine Academy. They would be enjoying their plates of beans and rice with clean water to drink. He recalled taking them for nature walks and playing outdoor games with them for his scouting project.

The little ones would hold his hands as they explored the mountain together. Their touch and trust in him made him feel loved in a very special way.

André asked God for strength. Strength to endure whatever happened to him.

The pickup lurched, jerking André out of his dream world. He realized he was kidnapped and unable to move.

The truck suddenly swerved to miss a rock pile. A gust of wind lifted the sack covering his head and blew it into the valley below. André could see inside the truck bed.

A wire cage dislodged from the corner of the pickup and slid within his view. Two beady eyes flashed. Something scratched to free itself.

André looked, "What is it? I'm not alone!"

…

Meanwhile Paul Robert ran as fast as he could to Sunshine Academy. The student assembly was about to begin. He hurried to Headmaster Thompson's office where Mr. Thompson was preparing the early morning worship service.

"Some men have kidnapped André," he explained. "They are in a blue pickup truck and looked headed for Les Cayes."

The Headmaster thanked Paul Robert and told him he would do what he could. He immediately picked up his cell and placed two calls. The first call was made to André's father and the next to a friend, Pastor Jackson, who lived in Les Cayes.

How do most Haitians travel?

Walking is the only transportation most Haitians can afford. Some farmers are fortunate to have donkeys and horses. Bicycles and motorbikes are popular, but expensive.

What is a tap-tap?

Tap-taps are vans and pick-up trucks with wooden benches. They are the primary means of transport within the cities.

People pile into them with all kinds of baggage...chickens, fruit, vegetables...to sell at the roadside markets.

Decorated with colorful religious and voodoo symbols, they are the most popular means of travel in Haiti. The dream of every child is to ride a tap-tap. When one arrives at his destination, he taps on the window and tells the driver to stop. The traveler pays for the distance traveled.

Poor road conditions and fuel costs limit the use of tap-taps in the rural areas of Haiti.

What is a hutia?

The Hispaniolan hutia (hoo-tee-ah) is a rodent-like animal about the size of a cat. It mainly inhabits trees.

Hunting at night, the hutia burrows into rough hillsides and ravines searching for roots and fruit. Hutia live in pairs and give birth to a single offspring. With its scaly tail, dense brownish or grayish fur and sharp claws, it is well-equipped for foraging and digging.

Today, the hutia faces extinction due to the devastation of their forest habitat and from being hunted for food.

3

The Hutia

André stared in disbelief at the trapped animal. He thought. "It's a hutia! It's a baby male hutia!" He watched it struggle to keep its balance. Its cage was a mess. Smashed fruit was everywhere. Its water bowl upside down. André thought, "What is a creature like that doing here?"

He remembered his grandmother's stories about the hutia, those pug-nosed, cat-sized inhabitants of Mount Macaya. They forage nightly for food. "Very few were kept for pets," his grandmother said. "They were meat. Not bad tasting. Sometimes we sacrificed them to the spirits at our voodoo temple. We fattened them with roots and fruit."

André recalled a young hutia captured on Mount Macaya by an American zoo keeper visiting the school when André was ten years old. He snapped a picture of André holding it. His mom framed the photo and hung it in the bedroom next to a portrait of Christ.

He remembered a Dr. Fontaine who spoke at his school assembly last year. The scientist declared that the hutia were dying fast. "Mount Macaya is their last refuge," he said. "We must protect them," he cautioned.

André whispered to the frightened animal. "Don't be afraid. I'll help you. Mind if I call you Hoot?" The little male hutia trembled.

The morning air was hot and humid. The pickup slowed to a crawl painfully passing through roads clogged with herds of goats, and pigs nosing into piles of garbage.

Dom nudged Couteau awake from his nap. "We should make it to Port-au-Prince tomorrow. We've got plenty of gasoline," he said.

By early afternoon they parked near a crossroad known locally as "the bus station" for tap-taps. Vendors selling all sorts of food and snacks encircled the area.

"I need a toilet," Andre yelled. Only one latrine appeared in sight, a shack of eroding cement blocks with no door or roof stood near a drainage ditch. It originally had been built as a convenience for tourists who frowned on going to the toilet in public.

Dom pulled to a stop. Couteau lifted André out of the truck and loosened his ropes. André hobbled into the ramshackled restroom. It gave him a sense of security.

Dom yelled, "Don't give me any trouble, and

I'll remove the ropes. We'll make this trip easier for you. You give me crap and I'll kill you. Understand?" André lowered his head and nodded.

André read the faded sign inside of the door. "For the convenience of travelers. Built in 1936 by Arnaud Construction Company." André thought, "It must have been built by my great-grandfather, François Arnaud."

Returning to the pickup, André looked up at Dom and asked, "May I feed the hutia?"

"You are not only to feed it, but water it and clean its cage, understand?" Dom replied. "That's solely your job." He handed him a banana, some bread, and a chunk of fried goat meat.

Couteau walked toward them carrying a carton of cigarettes and assorted bottles of rum, whiskey, water, and Coca-Cola. "Nothing like real food for the wicked!" He smirked.

Dom ate very little food. He preferred to drink. He beamed as he lifted a glass of rum and soda. Looking at his fake Rolex he said, "Time to roll!"

"Before we get started," Couteau began, "I've got a question to clear up, Dom. Is this trip mainly to get this hutia? Seems dumb to me."

Dom drawled. "Right. You are aware that our boss, Le Tigre, is dying? He's desperately ill."

Couteau replied "I knew he was crazy after we

smuggled that white tiger in from India, the one he shows to all his buddies during his weekend binges."

Dom continued, "Stop interrupting me. I'm talking about AIDS, man. He's dying."

"You know about the curse?"

"What curse?" Couteau asked as he flicked his cigarette ash out the window.

"He will never be well, until…"

"Until what?"

"Le Tigre believes that the spirit of his dead grandmother, Angeline, continues to be angry with him for marrying Madame Noir. She has put a curse on him. He is doomed to die."

"What does the hutia have to do with this?"

"Moogami, Tigre's voodoo priestess told him two weeks ago that Angeline's spirit will remove the curse if Le Tigre offers Papa Legba, our Voodoo God, the blood of a Haitian Hutia. Le Tigre is paying her a fortune for the ceremony.

"Madame Noir is furious about the money Moogami demands. But what can she do?"

"So that's why all this fuss for a hutia!" Couteau said.

"That's right. It's Le Tigre's last chance to live! We're wasting time. I'll tell you more when we camp for the night."

Dom turned the ignition key. He roared the engine and turned on the lights. The wheels screamed as the pickup lunged into the road.

Dom found a spot to camp. He curled up in the pickup cab, checked his pistol, placed a bottle of rum on the dash, and drifted into sleep, murmuring, "I'm too tired to talk anymore."

Couteau was on edge. Questions plagued his mind. "We've kidnapped a child. Does Dom realize we are in deep trouble?"

…

André fed the hutia and gently scooted him back in his cage. "Good night my little friend," he whispered.

Why are there so few trees in Haiti?

Haiti has lost 98% of its lush forest cover that it had in the early 1900's. The major reason is the continuous cutting down of trees to make cooking charcoal.

Now widespread erosion occurs in this once beautiful country, making it difficult for farming.

4

Robbed

The early morning sun peeked above Mount Macaya. Its warming light revealed an observation post and lab, manned by Doctors Pierre Fontaine and his wife Marie, Canadian scientists from Montreal. The Fontaines were members of an international environmental protection group, "Save Mount Macaya." They have lived on the mountain for two years.

Pierre and his wife are concerned about the continual cutting of trees on Mount Macaya. "Less than 2% of the forests remains," he lamented. "Our being here hasn't stopped this horrible scalping of trees. Soon this beautiful mountain will be totally naked!"

Marie worried about the disappearance of Hutia, small cat-sized rodents that once lived abundantly on Mount Macaya. She thought, "These lovable creatures have no protection. Hunted and starved for food, they are going the way of the dodo bird."

Marie picked up an overnight fax from Washington.

She frowned at her husband, "The Washington Post reports that we have the last remaining hutia in Haiti. Here, read this fax."

Pierre was busy writing his annual report that was due in Montreal the next week. He looked up from his pile of data. "Marie, we need more support for our free primary school for children whose parents pledge to stop cutting trees. Our last appeal for funds failed."

Marie said, "I must run now and see how our hutia are doing in the lab. It's been two days since I last checked on them. I'll be back in an hour. I need to review their progress." She grabbed her keys and rushed out.

The lab, an outdoor area, was caged to protect the hutia from poachers and other predators. It was a five-minute walk down the hill.

Pierre continued to study a recent survey map of the remaining Macaya forest area. He sighed, sipping his coffee.

He had lost thirty pounds since coming to Haiti.

Twenty minutes passed. Marie flung open the door. "Why back so soon?" Pierre asked.

Marie screamed, "The lock is broken! Our one baby male hutia is missing. Gone. Gone. That little one will die if we don't find it soon!"

"Did you check the staff quarters?" Pierre asked.

"You bet I did. That new lab assistant has cleaned out his locker and left without notice. I just knew he was up to no good and couldn't be trusted."

"He couldn't have gotten far." Pierre observed.

"Depends on when he snatched the animal." Marie answered.

Pierre jumped up. "I must alert the national police in Les Cayes."

Marie grabbed his cell phone from him. "No, not yet. Let's see what we can do here first."

She walked outside for a better cell connection, and called trusted friends for help. She would have to close the primary school for today.

Pierre followed her outside. "It's nine o'clock now, Marie!" He exclaimed. "We haven't much time."

He continued, "We'll offer a reward. We must prevent that animal from being smuggled out of the country. If not sold to a pet collector…" Then the horrible thought came to him… "There's always animal sacrifice. A rare animal is worth a lot of money in the spirit world."

He phoned his British research friends in the Dominican Republic, warning them to be on guard to protect their hutia preservation project.

"What a sad day!" Pierre glanced at his watch. "I must alert the village leaders!"

Strapping his cell phone to his belt and grabbing his high-powered German binoculars, Pierre climbed into his mud-caked four-wheeler, and roared off down the shortcut to the nearest village.

At the first open clearing he stopped to survey the landscape below. Focusing his binoculars, he watched a blue pickup loaded with furniture on the horizon, turning to the main road to Les Cayes.

Pierre wondered, "Could our hutia be in that pickup?" He picked up his cell phone to call his friends in Les Cayes. Maybe they could have the police check the pickup.

No answer. But he left them a voicemail message. He then phoned several other community leaders with the news about their missing hutia – including Headmaster Thompson at Sunshine Academy, who told him that their student André Arnaud was missing.

They decided to offer a financial reward for information leading to their whereabouts. They began to put their plan into action.

Does Haiti have cell phone service?

Today, most Haitians rely on low-cost, pre-paid cell phones for communication.

During the 2010 earthquake disaster in Port-au-Prince, cell phone coverage was essential in allowing international rescue organizations to coordinate emergency responses.

5

Blocked

Dom eased the pickup into the line of traffic to Les Cayes, unaware that Pierre Fontaine had spotted his truck from a distant hill. Dom nervously ate a cracker and checked the fuel gauge. "Full" he grinned. He had siphoned gas from his storage tank in the truck bed last night.

Couteau sucked on a cigarette, blowing smoke out the pickup's window. "We should be through Les Cayes soon," Dom said. "In Haiti I never leave anything to chance."

The heavy humidity signaled the day would be very hot. André had slept little. Mosquitos had swarmed over him most of the night. The heat sapped André's appetite.

Crammed in the bed of the pickup and no longer tied, André looked up to see the distant peak of Mount Macaya. Flashes of reflected sunlight blinked as if someone were signaling from the windows of the lab station.

The heat sapped André's appetite. He sipped water and nibbled a crust left from last night. Hoot lapped water and chewed small bits of bananas.

André recalled happily the weekends his father had brought him to the lab to watch the house and hutias while the Fontaines attended conferences in Port-au-Prince. He could snack and read in their library.

The main road became increasingly crowded with lines of homeless seeking work. Women rushed to claim ideal spots along the road to sell their vegetables and charcoal. Tap taps blared their horns in frustration.

Dom searched for openings in the traffic where he could accelerate from their snail-like speed. He was blocked by too many people with no place to go other than straight ahead.

Dom shifted into low gear. A goat crushed by a tourist bus lay dead in the road, its owner furiously demanding money for his loss.

Dom accelerated the pickup to dart around the accident.

The pickup crept slowly toward Les Cayes. Five kilometers before reaching the city, the endless chain of traffic stopped cold. Something was wrong. Very wrong.

"I'll check it out." Dom said. "You wait here, Couteau." Dom crawled out of the pickup and moved in closer. He saw a man pointing his semi-automatic for all to detour down a side road to be inspected. A peasant farmer who had tried to run lay wounded shot through the leg. Bleeding profusely, he begged for help.

A mother broke loose. Her basket of vegetables toppled from her head. Her terrorized child screamed. She shouted, "Bandits dressed like policemen are robbing us! Taking everything. Get away now!"

Forcing his way back through the crowd, Dom raced to the pickup. "We've got to get out of here fast. We must ditch the pickup. Couteau, unload the animal and Restavec. Grab our food, water bottles and guns. The rest we leave!"

"What about our license tag and car papers?" Couteau asked.

"They're all forged. Leave them to throw the police off. Let's go now!" Dom shouted.

Dom inched the pickup to the edge of a steep ravine, killed the motor, shifted the gears into neutral, and released the brakes. André, Dom and Couteau watched the pickup dive and flip to smash below, bottom up, tires spinning.

Dom wiped his hands on his shirt and retraced his steps to the trail. "It can't be seen from here. Let's go. We haven't much time."

Dom let André run carrying Hoot in a sling of

cleaning rags and made sure they had everything they needed for travel. He led the group up a rugged mountain path, sweeping his Luger pistol from side to side.

Again, Dom warned André, patting his Luger, "Don't ever think of trying to escape. I have a clip of bullets with your name on it."

He strapped his scoped rifle to his back. "Just in case," he said, "for any long distance work."

They jogged about three kilometers. The trail abruptly ended at a farmer's hut. Couteau retreated a short distance to make sure they were not followed. "We're okay." he reported.

Holding Hoot in his arms, André gasped and lay on his back, out of breath.

Dom scrapped his plans to reach Les Cayes. He must rethink what to do.

He thought the hutia must be delivered at all costs, and the restavac, well, if he didn't make it, he didn't make it.

A farmer abruptly appeared. Seeing the rifle, he became terrified. His wife and children peeked from their hut. Dom calmed them down, giving him a cigarette and chocolate to the wife and kids, and asked for their help to guide them to the coast.

Dom offered the farmer fifty US dollars to take them around Les Cayes to a fishing village on

Haiti's South Coast. The farmer complied willingly. Never had he received so much money at one time. One month of wages for a few days' work. And it was in American dollars, not gourdes. He crossed himself. He felt blessed and thanked the saints for this unexpected bounty.

Dom hoped to find a boat to take them east to Jacmel, a city large enough where he could rent a car to drive them safely to Port-au-Prince. Money was no problem. He worked for the richest gun-runner and drug dealer in Haiti. His wad of dollars impressed everyone. It bought immediate cooperation, but he worried incessantly of being robbed.

...

In Les Cayes, Pastor Jackson phoned troubling news to Headmaster Thompson at Sunshine Academy. "The pickup has been found five kilometers from here – wrecked, abandoned and completely stripped," he said. André's abductors had slipped away. Where was André? He didn't know. He prayed he was alive. He mentioned a broken cage was found with animal feces and hair.

Pastor Jackson tried to console Headmaster Thompson. "We'll keep our church members searching the port here and surrounding roads. We will never give up. Give my love to Henri."

Thompson examined his giant wall map of Haiti. "They've got to be somewhere near Les Cayes," he said. Thompson remembered André as one of his best Boy Scouts in his Sunshine Troop. He thought, "André has survival skills. He can make it through. They couldn't have gotten far."

...

The farmer guided them to a hilltop overlooking the sea. A small fishing village lay below. Dom reckoned they were about five kilometers west of Les Cayes. Boats rocked in the bay. The place seemed lifeless.

The farmer ushered them into a dimly lit hut overlooking the beach. André lay down with the hutia on the dirt floor in the corner.

The farmer introduced Dom and Couteau to his brother-in-law who staggered to the door, half asleep.

"Why no boats out today?" Dom asked the brother-in-law.

"Our mayor died. Funeral's this afternoon. What can I do for you?" he asked.

Dom arranged their passage for the next day with an offer that couldn't be refused. Four hundred U.S. dollars if they could reach Jacmel within three days, and eight hundred if they made it within two days. One-half to be paid immediately and the rest upon arrival. "Agreed," said the boat owner. "We sail at dawn tomorrow. You can stay here for the night for another fifty. Another twenty-five for some fish and rice."

Dom knew he was being cheated big time. He had sufficient money and it wasn't the right time to endanger their escape route by bargaining. Time was precious.

André considered how he might run away with Hoot. To try to escape now could be fatal. He must return Hoot to Mount Macaya alive. He realized it would be easier in Port-au-Prince, where he could find a safer place to be rescued. He remembered his father describing several mission schools.

"My biggest threat now is Dom," André thought. "Dom could be dangerous. After heavy drinking, he becomes a trigger-happy monster even randomly firing his Luger at insects!"

André remembered his Boy Scout experiences as a member of the Sunshine Academy Troop.

He recalled failing the fire building test for Second Class rank when his third match was wet and wouldn't light. He didn't pass because he had not prepared to succeed. He whispered to Hoot,

"I promise you I will be prepared and we will escape when the time is right."

What is voodoo?

Voodoo is a folk religion involving the worship of many gods and goddesses called "loas", each with separate powers.

Voodooism combines belief in West African deities, ancestral worship, and Roman Catholicism. Voodoo followers believe that the supreme Creator God "Bondye" is uninterested in one's everyday affairs so one needs to draw power from the Voodoo gods of this earth to improve one's life circumstances.

In order to gain these favors, an adherent participates in special Voodoo ceremonies accompanied with drumming, music, and gifts to the loa; usually including an invitation for loa to temporarily possess the adherent's body. This is called "mounting".

Bokors, in voodoo, are sorcerors, priests, or priestesses for hire that practice both black and light magic.

Their black magic includes the creation of 'zombies' and 'oaungas' (charms). A zombie is the reanimated body of a dead person controlled by evil forces. Light magic is practiced to do good.

6

So Close

The fishing boat slipped out into the Caribbean, its sails billowed by a gentle breeze. André marveled at the brilliant dawn. His first experience of early morning on the ocean.

André sat up and watched the parade of huts and shacks that came into view mile after mile, interrupted by luxurious hotels and homes snuggling around them.

André had never seen so many boats sail by. Some craft elegantly equipped with radar. One yacht, flying the Danish flag, carried a helicopter. Another bore the name the Belching Barge. Its deep sea fishing addicts swiveled in their chairs. They waved 'how lucky can we be?' holding their shot glasses high.

André thought of the days pirates infested these waters, planned their raids on defenseless villages and seized ships full of gold and luxurious jewelry bound for the thrones of Europe.

He glanced at Hoot, who had freed his tail from a fishing net. "I wish some pirates would come, but they would probably hold us for ransom," he sighed.

The fishing boat wallowed and pitched. André and Hoot both became seasick. Feeling weak and nauseous, André stretched out on some folded sails. Hoot snuggled under André. Couteau rushed to safety in the wheelhouse.

A freighter loaded with grain suddenly splashed into view, digging its deep furrow in the foaming sea. Its crew laughed and pointed at the small fishing boat struggling to keep upright and afloat.

The owner of the fishing boat became alarmed. His boat was out of control. "I've got to use our engine. Can't depend on the wind to pull us away from these big ships. They almost capsized us overboard." His companion went below and started the motor. The soft purr sent a sound of relief as they sped to safer waters.

Their boat threaded around Les Cayes and Île-à-Vache, a beautiful island south of the city. Remnants of an old fort popped up on the horizon. André was too sick to care about sightseeing. He felt terrible.

The fisherman brought some strange leaves to André. "Chew these." You'll feel better." André gagged on them, then felt better and fell asleep. The boat churned forward peacefully.

Mid-afternoon, the fisherman's brother yelled. "Everybody awake! We have a police patrol bearing down on us!"

Dom became nervous. "We may have to shoot our way out of this one." He unlocked the safety on his rifle. He counted a platoon of seven. "They could overtake us in an instant," he said.

Their sailors stood ready to board.

Dom screamed, "Couteau, hide the restavec and animal. Now! They must not be seen."

Dom crossed himself and set his Luger for rapid fire. "Mary, Mother of Jesus, protect us!"

André and Hoot were shoved under a tarp. Dom yelled, "One sound from either of you, and I'll put some hot lead into your stomachs."

Couteau kissed the barrel of his pistol. "And I'll blow both your heads off," Couteau shouted.

André blanched, speechless. He held Hoot close to his chest. His heart pounded.

The fishermen looked helplessly at one another. One rubbed a voodoo charm hanging from his neck.

A hundred yards away, the patrol craft veered and crossed within a few feet of the bow of the fishing boat firing its machine guns at a yacht 300 yards starboard.

"Whew!" Dom sweated. "So close!"

Couteau staggered to his feet and retrieved a bottle of rum. "They must be after a drug-runner because they didn't get their cut," he slurred. "Let's drink to that."

He passed the bottle around to Dom and to the fishermen who wobbled to control the rudder and lower their speed.

Gasping for air and dragging Hoot, André crawled out from under the canvas sail.

He petted Hoot. "Are you okay?" he asked.

Hoot wagged his tail and snuggled close to André.

What is the life expectancy in Haiti?

Due to improved nutrition, education, and medical care, life expectancy in Haiti has risen from 42 in 1960 to 62 in 2011. Though improved, this is 17 years shorter than the average person living in the U.S. Forty-two percent (42%) of Haiti's 10 million residents are children under the age of 18.

7

The Singing Angels Car Palace

The fishing boat bucked past long stretches of rocky beaches. Paths disappeared into the dense vegetation. Donkeys and horses were sighted pulling carts of charcoal and vegetables.

They sailed for several hours. Suddenly, gale force winds blew over the seas. They hammered their small craft. Their propeller spun uselessly in mid-air, unable to move the craft forward.

The captain yelled at the wheelhouse, "Head to the beach of Aquin! We've got to get out of here or we will drown!" Winds lashed out, whipping everything around with drenching rain.

The crew boss feared they would capsize. He switched on his submersible pump in the hold below. They were taking on too much water. The level subsided and they relaxed! They circled a rocky reef. The storm ceased to a light rain and calm water.

They entered the Bay of Aquin. Dom squinted

his eyes at the coastal road lined with clusters of palm trees and cell towers. He sighed with relief. "Coast is clear. No police."

He texted on his cell phone to Le Tigre. "We're about 8 hours from Jacmel. Should land there tonight. Travel is about 3 knots an hour. Sea still unpredictable. We'll be in touch."

Rounding Cape Jacmel, the ocean settled into a peaceful lake. They turned north into the bay. Dom ordered the fishermen to dock near the main road west of the town of Jacmel. Rows of shacks came into view with their colorful display of tee shirts, underwear, and bedding drying in the sun.

"I'm hungry," André exclaimed, admiring the rows of tropical fruit in the distance.

Dom commanded, "Get closer to those tap-taps over there."

"No problem," said the fisherman. He accelerated the speed until they docked.

Dom peeled out their fare, plus a bonus for their early arrival, and paid the boat owner.

A canary yellow tap-tap named "Sweet Jesus' Chariot" lay surrounded by a crowd squirming to board. The vehicle sagged from overloading. A goat, stuck in an inside seat, bleated to be rescued.

Another taxi screeched to a stop nearby. It bore the name "Dream Baby Dream" painted on its hood. Haloed angels strumming harps and reclining on white clouds decorated its side doors. Its driver leaned out. "Need a ride?" he asked.

Dom yelled, "We'll take it." Couteau and André carrying Hoot jumped aboard. Dom sat next to the driver. "Take us to the nearest car-dealer," he directed. "We need reliable transportation to Pétionville."

"I know just where to go," smiled the driver.

The taxi zigzagged madly through a maze of honking traffic and dodging pedestrians.

A kilometer later it squealed up to the Singing Angels Car Palace. A tin-roofed garage bore a large sign "Every Car Blessed by Angels! Bargains! Bargains! Bargains!"

The car salesman, wearing a cowboy hat covered with pin-on souvenir medals of U.S. states, cautioned Dom away from the line of cars in the front lot to his inside show room. "You don't want any of that junk." he said. He led Dom to a 1998 Toyota Blue Rav-4. "Just came in today from Miami. Don't mind the dent and bullet-hole. It runs well. Has 300,000 miles. Only $20,000 U.S. dollars."

Dom didn't have time to waste. He checked the motor. After bargaining back and forth he peeled $15,000 cash from his wad of $100 bills.

As they hurried to leave the dealer, Couteau

noticed the national TV blaring the latest news. A picture of a hutia flashed into view with the words below 'Endangered hutia stolen from Mount Macaya Science Lab. Reward for safe return of animal. Call Professor Fontaine at...' and the message trailed off.

"Did you see what I saw?" Couteau asked Dom. They immediately forced Hoot and André down on the back seat floor of the Rav, and covered them with their jackets.

Dom snarled, "One sound out of you and it's all over, understand? You and that animal stay hidden and quiet." André nodded. He feared for his life.

Dom glanced at Couteau, "We're going to Le Tigre's by the back roads now. Main roads north are too dangerous." Dom steered the Rav-4 east on the coastal road to the seaport of Marigot.

What is the weather like in Haiti?

The temperature in Haiti averages between 81 and 86 degrees Fahrenheit, with high temperatures about ten degrees warmer. The humidity, however, changes greatly throughout the year, so it often feels much warmer than it is actually measured to be.

The humidity and rainfall vary greatly throughout different parts of Haiti. Average rainfall in some mountain areas is over fifty inches per year while there are some spots which receive little rainfall at all. There are two rainy seasons. The first rainy season takes place in late spring and the other comes in the fall. From December through April, it is usually dry and less humid so many people prefer to travel to Haiti at this time.

8

Gates of Hell

Dom drove the 25-kilometer trip from Jacmel to Marigot in two and a half hours. Washed out sections and countless potholes kept their Rav to a speed of less than ten kilometers an hour.

"The last thing we want is for some local to see the restavec and the hutia together and report them. People will do anything for that reward money," said Dom.

André whimpered, "We can't breathe." Couteau replaced their jackets with old newspapers.

To relieve his discomfort, André counted pothole bumps. He quickly gave up. They continued forever.

Reaching Marigot a sign greeted them. "Haiti's Fishing Paradise."

"That reminds me," Couteau said, "Let's stop for lunch. I want some fried fish."

"We'll buy something to eat on the way. Can't linger. Too dangerous! We must reach Le Tigre's before sundown." Dom braked the Rav. "Toilet stop," he shouted. They relieved themselves behind a fish merchant's shack.

They entered an open-air cafe. Dom forked out five dollars. "Fry mine well done." He relished the taste of grease.

"Same for me," Couteau smacked his lips.

Couteau handed André a skimpy portion of fish, potatoes, and a bottle of water for him and the hutia. Being imprisoned on the hot floor had sapped their appetites.

Making a left and turning up a main mountain road, Dom said, "Here's the plan. Couteau, should we be stopped, make sure the restavec and hutia are out of sight. If they're discovered, we'll fight it out! Shoot to kill!"

Dom's goal was to reach the village of Furcy by mid-afternoon. There they would turn north into Kenscoff and wind their way into elite Pétion-ville, dominated by Le Tigre's fortress-mansion.

As Dom mounted a steep incline, a group of rag-tag children jumped on the back of the Rav to enjoy a free ride. Dom braked...and cursed at them. Couteau beat them off. They ran away laughing.

The Rav snaked around the mountains, weaving back and forth. The road was extremely dangerous to drive after a fresh rain. Dom knew that one slip of the wheels and they could plunge to certain death.

Skid marks deeply imprinted in the mud near

the road's edge revealed horrible accidents. Several smashed cars lay rusting in ravines below, too mangled to be safely salvaged.

Swaths of vacant land witnessed the devastation of floods in and around Marigot. The hurricanes pushed masses of soil with its sheets of pounding rain. Dom constantly shifted gears from second to low. The speedometer recorded zero to 5 kilometers per hour.

Patches of shanty towns appeared ringed by road stands of empty boxes. Faded umbrellas shaded mounds of bananas.

Ahead Cabaio Mountain, 2,282 feet above sea level, revealed its summit above a low bank of clouds that floated slowly toward Parc La Visite. The Rav's engine strained to climb a steep hill.

Reaching the top, Dom began the descent. The Rav skidded across a slick, muddy patch. The small car rocked from one sharp turn to another, then slid uncontrollably. André feared they would all die.

Dom crunched into second gear. He pulled the hand brake hard to stop the skid. "Nothing," he sweated. "I heard something snap as we climbed that last hill," he said.

Dom shifted into first. "No wonder they sold us this car in Jacmel. It's a piece of junk. The hand brake is now our downhill gears!" he complained.

The Rav coughed its way up past the Mountain Mission at Fermathe all the way to Kenscoff village, dotted with small vegetable gardens. The altitude cooled. André could breathe more easily.

Before them lay Pétionville, which overlooked the massive plain of Port-au-Prince, still reeling from the earthquake of 2010.

André raised himself to peek at the pristine mansions, magnificently poking their roofs of splendor above the hilly landscape. Shanty slums clung desperately to the slopes beneath this opulent display of wealth. Couteau observed. "Thank God for cheap labor. We couldn't live without it."

"And don't forget the demands for drugs, booze, and sex." Dom added. He puffed a lopsided smoke ring. " We supply them all."

Dom drove through a maze of high walled houses, adorned by floral trees and barbed wire. Buckets of flowers extended from window-sills. Guards stood armed near elaborate entrances. The scene resembled a mountain range topped by French chateaus. Wealth was on display everywhere.

Dom rounded a corner climbing to Pétionville's highest summit. There, LeTigre's fortress-mansion loomed majestically. Its massive round watchtower with a giant yellow pennant flapped the image of a leaping white tiger.

"Ah! We're home." Dom lay back from the driver's wheel. He beeped the horn.

Two heavy gates studded with steel nails slowly opened. Armed guards rushed toward the Rav. A sentry yelled "Bien Venue. Welcome!" to Dom from a bullet-proof sentry post.

Dom sighed, "It's time for us to rest in this little bit of heaven, Couteau." He stretched his arms upward and yawned.

André crawled out of the Rav holding Hoot still in its sling. His legs ached from being cramped for hours and Hoot had urinated on him.

André smelled awful. His clothes were ripped and dirty, and he was hungry.

He didn't know he and Hoot were passing through the gates of Hell.

What languages are spoken in Haiti?

Both French and Haitian Creole are official languages in Haiti. Creole is spoken by nearly everyone and is the language of choice for most situations, with the exception of weddings and funerals which are normally presided over in French.

Though French is taught in schools, less than 10% speak French fluently -- usually only the wealthy.

9

The Noose Narrows

Headmaster Thompson of Sunshine Academy phoned Pierre Fontaine, at the Macaya Mountain Research Station. "Good news, Pierre, I'm in Les Cayes. We just got a nibble regarding the information about your hutia and our André. A fisherman phoned. Said he had information that would interest us, but refused details until he's paid."

Pierre replied, "Great news. I'll send Marie down to see you. She's fluent in Creole. Where do you want to meet the fisherman?"

"Let's meet him at the church office in Les Cayes. You're fading out. I can barely hear you."

Fontaine raised his voice.

"Okay, it's clearer now! One o'clock." Thompson added, "Lunch included."

"Sure, Thompson. Marie's leaving now. She'll come alone."

Thompson clicked off.

Fontaine continued, "Oh, by the way, I can't leave

here. Don't want our hutia to disappear. Thanks for your prayers. Goodbye, and God bless you."

Fontaine realized his last remarks went unheard. He felt foolish as he shoved his cell back into his belt.

Marie met Thompson a half hour late. It was now two o'clock. "Held up by traffic," she said, catching her breath.

Thompson smiled. "Marie, there's been a further development. A woman west of Les Cayes called. She too offered information. Turns out she's a mayor's wife who says she saw André with the hutia a few days ago. She said her relative carried a boy with an animal.

"I cancelled the fisherman interview and asked her to meet with us. She's taking the next tap-tap she can get. Should be here in a couple of hours. Are you hungry?"

Della, Thompson's wife, served them peanut butter-jelly sandwiches and cold limeade. "Will you spend the night with us?" she asked Marie.

"We'll see how late our meeting goes," Marie replied.

At five o'clock, a plump heavy-set woman stood at the Thompson's office door.

"Please come in," Thompson said.

She carried a basket of fish and pineapples on

her head. She wore a traditional wrap-around skirt printed with Bible verses in rainbow colors topped with a white blouse. Her shoes were blue canvas, with no socks. She carried a baby granddaughter sucking a bottle. She grinned proudly.

"You said you had information about our missing student and the hutia."

"Oui, monsieur." Her baby began to cry. She had wet her diaper. The woman held the baby out away from her.

Thompson sensed that French was difficult for her. He replied in Creole, "You may speak in Creole."

He introduced himself and then Marie.

"Professor Fontaine is fluent in Creole. Please sit down."

Thompson looked at his visitor. "Please relax. You are with friends. What is your name?"

"Hadriana."

"Where do you live?"

"A small fishing village west of Les Cayes."

Thompson said, "Let's have a cool drink." Fresh limeade was served. Hadriana fed some to the baby, who gurgled with contentment.

Marie looked at Hadriana. "I want to buy your fish and pineapples. How much?"

Bargaining followed, with Hadriana happy to receive more dollars than she expected. Marie handed her purchases to Thompson. "Would you put these in your fridge? Please keep half for you and Della."

"Now back to your information, Hadriana. Once we have heard your facts, we can determine the amount of your reward. Understand?"

"Yes."

"Go ahead."

"About five days ago I saw my brother-in-law load the hutia and boy onto his fishing boat. His wife told me they were going to a beach just west of Jacmel. That's all I know."

"What's the name of the boat?"

"La Reine, The Queen."

For the next half hour, Hadriana answered all questions put to her by Thompson and Marie. She seemed sincere and trustworthy.

"This helps us greatly, Hadriana. We'll be back in a minute." Marie and Thompson retired to another room. They returned with an envelope of dollars.

Hadriana was delighted. The reward was more than she anticipated. She thanked them with Creole caresses and kisses, then left to catch a tap-tap back to her village before night shrouded the southern coast. The baby had wet again but she carried a nice supply of clean diaper cloths, compliments of the mission clinic.

Thompson and Marie phoned their friends in Jacmel to comb the west beaches for the fishing boat, The Queen. They didn't know that André and the hutia had already arrived at Le Tigre Mansion in Pétionville.

Do children watch television in Haiti?

Most families in Haiti cannot afford a television and have limited access to electricity.

In major cities, it is not uncommon today, however, to find people gathered around a TV set inside a home or set up outside, especially during soccer season.

10

Imprisoned

The Rav eased into the outer courtyard. Two men in military dungarees closed the entry gates. Another guard exited a sentry box atop the front wall, covering every movement of Dominique and Couteau. Looking up Dom said, "Hey, we're okay. You can call the hounds off. We work here, you know."

A voice shouted from the second story balcony. "They're okay. Le Tigre's expecting them."

Couteau yanked André out of the van. He led him to Madame Noir, who was sipping gin and swinging in a hammock. "Bring the restavec closer," she ordered. She tossed her Paris fashion magazine to the floor and sat up to peer over her designer sunglasses for a better look.

She slipped on her sequined flip-flops, stood up and walked around André, who held the hutia, hidden in a sling.

"It should do all right." She pulled his ears. "Good color and muscles. Looks hungry. Needs a bath."

She pinched his private parts. André cried "Ouch! That hurts!"

Madame slapped André. "Don't make a sound until I ask for an answer. Understand?

"And where's Le Tigre's hutia?" She asked.

Couteau removed the sling from André. It's here." He pulled the squirming animal out to view.

"Put it in the cage in the kitchen. Have the restavec water and feed it. It must be kept alive for now." She grinned. Her gold front tooth flashed.

Le Tigre, shakily supported by crutches, limped into the room. His hair was disheveled. He barely spoke above a whisper. He patted the frightened hutia. "My ancestor's spirit should be pleased. I can be cured. Won't be long now."

He glanced at André and then toward Madame. "I see you've received my gift - a restavec for you," he said.

"Yes, thank you, my dear. So thoughtful of you."

Le Tigre continued. "He's an orphan, Couteau told me. Abandoned victim of a fire. I got him free. Name's André."

André looked down. "Abandoned. No way!" he thought. "I was kidnapped. Couteau's lying. My dad's alive."

Madame Noir looked at Le Tigre. "Great! I have some rules and jobs for it."

"Look at me," she ordered André. She hit him. Her diamond ring slashed his cheek. Bleeding, André screamed in pain.

Madame Noir wacked him again. "Now look what you've done!" she yelled. "You've bled on my nice clean dress. Shame on you!"

She stared at André. "Here your name is Restavec, not André. Do you hear me?"

André crouched on the floor.

"You are lucky to have food and a place to stay. Get up. Come with me. I'll show you where you sleep and eat and the work you're to do."

André stood up, wobbly and hungry.

They passed Hoot lapping water from a bowl. The cook pushed food into its cage. André's eyes met those of his little friend for a brief moment.

"This way." Madame shoved André toward the cleaning closet.

They stopped at a small storage room. Papers and rags were scattered about. Mops and a frazzled broom leaned in the corner. Cans of dried soap powder and dirty brushes lay crusted to a mildewed shelf.

Madame gestured toward a worn-out blanket and ripped pillow on the floor.

"This is your bed. Our last guest wasn't very tidy. You'll do better, I'm sure. There's a change of clothing for you." She motioned toward a faded tee shirt and a tattered Chicago White Sox baseball cap hanging on a nail. Ragged blue denim shorts lay nearby. None had been washed for weeks.

"Over there's your toilet. The cook uses it, so keep it clean." It was a hole in the floor with two raised places for feet. Madame's old magazines with slick pages served for toilet paper.

"Next, your meals." They walked into the dining area near the kitchen. "You are allowed to eat only after everyone else has eaten. Food and water will be left out for you on this corner table.

"There's some here for you. Eat. I'll return in a few minutes, then we'll go over your work schedule."

André sat down to small scraps of leftover breakfast of half-eaten bread and papaya. "How cruel can people be?" he asked himself.

He stared at a crucifix hanging on the kitchen wall. The statue of Christ seemed to writhe in pain. Below it stood a table decorated with a bowl of Madame's handwritten prayer requests.

A candle flickered. "This is crazy," André thought.

Who were the first Protestant missionaries in Haiti?

After the great slave revolt of 1791 and the island's subsequent independence from France in 1804, the Roman Catholic Church was declared to be the state church of Haiti.

Colonial policy had forbidden Protestantism. It was not until 1816 that the first Protestants were permitted to enter the country to openly proclaim their version of the Gospel of Jesus Christ.

In 2010, now nearly half the country considers themselves to be Protestant.

11

The White Tiger

'Tigre' Noir suffered another rough night. His aching body wasted away more rapidly now. Drugs seemed incapable of reducing his incessant pain.

Madame Noir had cautioned her husband, "Never invite your cronies for a night of cards and drinking. You're too weak and too sick to have such a party. It will only make you worse."

Le Tigre ignored her. He was anxious to throw a party his friends would never forget.

It was Friday night. Haiti's elite gangsters arrived in their Mercedes and Cadillacs. One rode up in his Rolls Royce escorted by bodyguards.

Le Tigre invited them to ascend on his private elevator to a room in the mansion's tower. A huge yellow pennant of a leaping white tiger fluttered from a pole above the roof. In this tower Noir housed his 'pride and joy,' an exotic pet. It was a huge male white tiger.

The magnificent animal lay chained surrounded by goat bones and chunks of spoiled beef. A cement trench circulated a constant flow of water.

Noir ceremoniously unlocked the tiger room door for his guests to view his rare creature and laughingly declared, "Meet my friend, Siber." He relished in their astonished looks.

Noir believed his tiger had been captured in Siberia and then sold on the international black market of rare animals.

Noir's cronies accepted his claim that the Tiger was rare, but not from Siberia. They had been involved in the deal to smuggle it into Haiti at great cost to Noir. They knew that it was an inbred Bengal from India and a black and white striped genetic weakling that ended up in a Las Vegas show.

The tiger was now retired from years of a cracking whip, treats of bite-sized meats, and jumping through rings of fire. When the tiger became unpredictable and turned vicious, it was sold to the highest bidder. False breeding documents fooled Noir into buying it.

Noir summoned Richard, Siber's full-time caretaker.

"Meet Ree-Char," Noir announced. "He's Siber's caretaker."

Noir asked Ree-Char, "Has Siber been fed today?"

Ree-Char lied. "Fed? He's gorged and sluggish."

Ree-Char actually was selling half of Siber's

meat to friends and relatives. The animal was continually hungry and dangerous.

Noir approached Siber. He ran his fingers across its furrowed brow and slowly fluffed its arched back of wiry fur, then scratched its ears. The big cat raised its paw, extending its razor sharp claws. It snarled, uncovering its massive fangs.

Noir withdrew his hand. "I don't believe Siber wants to play with me today," he said. "It's best we go now." Noir ushered his guests into the hallway.

He turned to Ree-Char. "After we leave, unchain Siber. Take him for a walk. He seems sleepy."

Ree-Char bowed. "Your wish is my command, Sir."

The entourage descended on the private elevator. A guest asked, "Tigre, is your cat a man-eater? Is he dangerous?"

"Not if you know how to manage him. Siber's well-fed and exercised. I have a local vet check him every six months."

Another friend quizzed him. "Have you reported to the government authorities you have a pet tiger in your home?"

Noir responded with an "air" of confidence, sucking an unlit Havana cigar. "I'm supposed to, but I pay 'fees' to the local officials and government vet to say nothing."

After a tense night of heavy betting, Noir edged

his guests to the front entrance. Their gleaming luxury cars, with drivers and body guards, awaited them in the courtyard.

The cook's daughter set glasses on a hallway table.

Noir invited them to gather around. "One for the road, gentlemen. What's your pleasure?" he asked.

They toasted each other good night. Noir laughed as they departed, "May your dreams be bullet-proof."

Noir painfully climbed the stairs to his bedroom. "These crutches are killing me. I must extend the elevator to the ground floor," he promised himself.

The Noirs slept through the night blanked-out by liquor. Neither bothered to lock their doors.

Dawn's first light peeked through the third floor skylight.

It was 6 a.m. Ree-Char rolled out of bed to check on Siber.

He found Siber's door open. The room was empty.

He rushed downstairs into Tigre's bedroom and shook him awake.

"Master, Siber has escaped. He's on the loose. Roaming the place. We are in danger."

Noir, still semi-sedated from alcohol, stammered to clear his mind. "F-F-Find him. Don't k-k-kill Siber. G-G-Get Dom and C-C-Couteau to help you."

Noir sat up. He looked terrible. His eyes were bloodshot. He cautioned, "And for God's sake, don't tell Madame Noir. She would become ballistic…mad…crazy! Lock her door and let her sleep."

"I'll lock your door, Master. Rest easy," Ree-Char said and ran out the room.

Ree-Char locked all outside doors.

Dom and Couteau lived in the guard's quarters inside the mansion. Ree-Char alerted them on the intercom.

They met Ree-Char in the main hallway and decided they would search for Siber together, beginning with the top floor down.

Armed with automatic AK rifles for distance targets and handguns for close range, they stealthily searched for Siber's trail. Dom clutched his German Luger, his finger itching on the trigger.

They scoured the guest suites, supply closets, the arsenal, the interrogation lab, TV/movie room, the bar, the card room, and the "internet command center". "No luck, so far," lamented Dom.

At the far end of the second floor hall lay the main entrance to the Noir Family Worship Center – divided into the Temple of Legba and a Prayer Chapel.

Couteau found the Prayer Chapel door bolted shut. Dom turned toward the Temple entrance. Its entry door ajar, just enough for Siber to squeeze through. Tiger droppings lay just inside.

The three stalkers eased into the Legba Temple, each deathly scared. A candle flickered over a gleaming razor-sharp machete. Voodoo art in brilliant colors adorned the walls. The place smelled like a morgue. An altar table exhibited freshly painted voodoo symbols and gods.

A goat's skull vibrated the message "Intruders Beware." A ten-foot high ledge encircled the worship area.

The eerie atmosphere made Dom feel extremely uneasy. He felt he had interrupted a sacred ceremony.

Ree-Char screamed. A flash of black and white stripes from above crushed him into the floor. His rifle bounced and fired into the ceiling.

Dom wheeled, shooting at this black and white terror tearing Ree-Char to bits. His back had been instantly broken by the massive weight of a mad tiger.

Dom emptied his clip into the enraged cat.

Couteau fired into the animal's chest, to lay his claim to contributing to the death of a savage beast already dead.

Salvos of gunfire brought the Noirs out of their rooms. Tigre Noir hobbled painfully between Madame Noir and his crutch. Both were ashen-faced with fear.

Dom said, "We hated to kill Siber, boss, but we had no choice."

Noir looked down. His pajamas soaking wet with sweat. "Ree-Char was a good man. Faithful. I hate to see him die this way."

He continued, "As for my beautiful pet, I guess you can take the tiger out of the jungle, but never the jungle out of the tiger."

Madame comforted her husband. "Noir, I'll have Siber stuffed as a memorial to Ree-Char. You'll have Siber as long as you live.

"And one more thing. Siber's heart and genitals will sell for big prices on the black market. We might make as much as $50,000. We've got work to do. I'll get Restavec to clean this mess up. He's probably in the kitchen."

...

André was enjoying an unusual breakfast, a dirty glass of fizzless Coca-Cola and a crumpled bag of chips trashed by Madame Noirs' children. His euphoria was short-lived.

Madame spotted him. She charged into the room waving her 'correction stick.'

Do all children attend school in Haiti?

Sadly, only about half of Haitian children finish elementary school, resulting in only 50% of Haiti's population to be literate. With few public schools, most parents cannot afford to pay the cost of entrance fees, tuition, books, uniforms, and school supplies.

Child education sponsorship programs offered through organizations, such as Hope for Haiti's Children, allow children from impoverished homes or orphans to receive a quality private education.

12

No School
for the Pig

André's first week in the Noir household was a living hell. How long could he endure? He thought of the many children he had seen wandering the streets whose father or mother had died of AIDS, the same sickness sucking the life out of "Le Tigre" Noir.

Aside from lack of food and sleep, André's endurance was severely tested by the Noir's two spoiled children. Son, Michael, age fifteen, and Beatrice, age thirteen, were addicted to texting on their cell phones. Beatrice's wardrobe overflowed with Parisian sunglasses. Michael stole his father's British cigarettes. Both took their mother's drugs to endure their weekends of boredom.

The Noir children spilled food and drink on the floor daily, demanding André to clean it up. They hid his cleaning supplies, rags, and mops. They sprinkled tacks in his blanket.

Madame Noir caught them sticking chewing

gum under the dining room chairs. They blamed André. But Madame knew better. She wacked both with her 'correction stick.' André felt a moment of relief. Then she turned on him and beat him for no reason other than he was a restavec.

André's most painful moment with the teenagers came each morning as they marched out in their immaculate blue and white Saint Mary's School uniforms. They carried their satchels of books mostly unread and unopened. André felt jealous and hurt.

Before boarding the family limo that drove them to school, they yelled at André. "No school for the dummy today! No school for the restavec!"

Each weekday afternoon the Noir's two teenagers tromped in from school, a private one on the main road below, run by Catholic nuns. They plopped their books down hard on the kitchen table to intimidate André.

One evening André had fed Hoot, and was on his knees cleaning up the mess the two had made at breakfast.

"Too bad you can't go to school. They don't allow animals to attend," the daughter taunted.

"Your clothes stink!" Her brother added, squashing an orange into the floor. André longed for an orange and to see one wasted sickened him.

André didn't look up. He kept brushing the soap-suds over the black spots and rinsing the dirty rag in a bucket of cold water.

"Hey! I'm talking to you. Look at me, thing," the brother ordered. Then he kicked André, flipped over the bucket and threw the scrub brush out the window.

André painfully rose. The children chanted, "Look at our pet pig, pet pig, pet pig. Oink, oink!"

Madame Noir charged into the kitchen. "What's going on?" She yelled. Her daughter, Beatrice, pointed to the overturned bucket. "What are you going to do about this mess, mother?" Beatrice marched out of the room, not waiting for an answer.

Madame Noir stared at her son. "You're behind this. Leave my restavec alone. It's my property. Let it do its work." She blocked her son from leaving and cuffed him hard up side his head. Holding his cheek, he turned toward André and sobbed, "I'll get you for this. You pig!"

"Go do your homework!" Madame screamed.

"I'll deal with your sister later."

"I hate you, Mother." Her son's voice faded as he ran into the courtyard.

André blinked. For a moment he felt that perhaps Madame Noir would treat him more kindly. She had punished her son for cruelty. She seemed approachable.

One afternoon André observed Madame to be in one of her better moods. He approached her submissively. He proposed she allow him to tutor her children in French. He overheard they were failing. He explained he would do this in addition to all his other chores.

Madame exploded. "You're trying to get out of work, Restavec. My children don't like you. And neither do I. Now get back to that patio floor. Once a restavec, always a restavec. Understand?"

She clipped André's head hard with a kitchen tablespoon.

"You only speak when I give you permission. You are not my child. In fact, I don't see you as a child. Why am I listening to you? After you clean the floor, dump the garbage outside in the ditch and..." The upstairs bell rang.

She gulped a shot of rum and poured a fresh one. "It's Le Tigre wanting his afternoon 'Nectar of the Gods'." She called the cook to carry it up to him.

Never again did André make such an offer. He became more resolved than ever to get Hoot and run.

The cook slowly climbed the spiral staircase to Le Tigre's room. She was sad. She had just witnessed André's hopelessness. She thought, "Perhaps I can help André somehow."

One afternoon the Noir children, back from school, announced they had a gift for André. Beatrice pointed at André, "It's Dummy Day!"

"And you're it!" Michael plopped a dunce cap on André.

They got the idea from watching a TV history film on Mao Tse-Tung's Red Brigade Army torturing American-educated Chinese.

André left the room. He tore the cap to shreds and dropped them in the kitchen toilet.

André had excelled as a scholar at Sunshine Academy. He finished first in French every year. His father Henri dreamed of the day his son might be a professor in Port-au-Prince. He knew he could help Beatrice and Michael if they accepted him as a human being. But they denied him his humanity.

André now knew the cold, heartless reality he was forced to endure. "How long can I last?" he asked himself. He prayed a flash prayer, "Please help me, Jesus."

He glanced at Hoot cowering in a corner of his cage on the back veranda. Hoot was growing weaker each day.

André ached to be free.

That night, after Le Tigre's guard dogs had quieted down, André lay back, his hands behind his head, wondering what next to do. One week remained before the full moon, the time for the voodoo ceremony and sacrifice of his little friend. He had to leave soon if he and Hoot were to stay alive.

How are Christians bringing hope to Haiti's children?

Christian missions and faith-based non-government organizations (NGO's) provide a majority of the schools, health clinics, water wells, and feeding programs in Haiti.

The future of Haiti lies in its youth. Hope for a better life is possible as these children are taught the eternal importance of each individual in God's sight along with truthfulness, integrity, and justice for all – resulting in morally upright and wise Haitian leaders of tomorrow.

13

The Note
With the Necklace

Madame's Napoleon wall clock rang eleven times. The city electric power had shut down. Workers were on strike. They demanded a living wage. The Noir back-up generator lay idle, out of fuel. The diesel delivery service called to say they were delayed for the next two days.

Madame prepared for her usual end-of-the-day shower. She imagined herself to be a modern-day Marie Antoinette and had ordered her powder room repainted pink.

Madame had the habit of thoroughly soaping and lathering her hair before she stepped into a soothing stream of warm, refreshing rinse. She turned the golden wall knob to her preferred mix of hot with cold.

No water. Not even a drop. She was furious, with no one to call! The cook had gone home to her shack down the hill. At night it was too dangerous to send her restavec to a municipal tap, a half-mile away. He could be kidnapped by another family.

Across the hall her husband, Le Tigre, lay helpless in a trance from a painkiller, a potion given by his voodoo priestess.

Madame Noir mopped her soggy coiffure with a heavy towel, gritted her teeth, and exclaimed. "Haiti, curse you. You win again. I want to move to Miami!"

She toweled herself dry, slipped into her black satin dressing gown with matching eye mask and dropped on top of her bedding, emotionally drained.

…

Pétionville, dotted by well-lit mountain mansions settled into the black night. Drums thumped. Police sirens pierced the strange rhythms in the distance. It was a typical night for the anxious poor huddled in shacks. They longed for the safety of morning light.

André crawled into his makeshift bed of cardboard and rags, covered by a threadbare quilt. Andre had endured a hard day. He curled up, rolled a dirty sugar sack into a pillow. He itched. He was too exhausted to scratch.

Just after one a.m., a sliver of moonlight peeked through the small barred window of the storage room where André lay gazing into the darkness.

Startled by the light, André awoke.

His gaze followed its beam to a hole in the wall. A paper rolled like a scroll stuck out. He sat up and pulled it out.

Inside he found a tiny gold necklace and a penciled note written in Creole. It read: "The Noirs are going to kill me. Whoever receives this note and my mother's necklace, tell my Uncle Vincent Lavalier in Miragoâne I love him with all my heart. Signed Émile Francois Rousseau."

André put the note and cross back into the hole.

He thought, "Émile must be the boy who died at the police station. I'm replacing him."

André sighed. "Miragoâne is two hours by tap-tap, west of Port-au-Prince."

If he found Émile's uncle, would he help him return to Macaya?

Why are music and dance important in Haiti?

Music and dance express the soul of the nation. They provide a joyous release from day-to-day struggles and oppressive poverty.

West African and French colonial influences combine into distinctly Haitian music and rhythm.

The fundamental instrument in Haiti is a drum, crafted into various sizes and shapes. One of Haiti's most unique musical instruments is the "mosquito drum." It resembles a one-string harp.

14

The Temple of Legba

André had been a slave in the Noir Mansion for a week. It was a nightmare! He yearned to escape Madame Noir's constant cruelty. He wanted to throw her 'correction stick' into the fire.

Hoot lost weight daily. His confined living space pressed in on him. No exercise and lack of proper diet of mountain roots and plants had taken a toll.

André had to find a way out soon. He heard Madame say, "Next Saturday is the full moon and time for Legba to reach the Supreme Healer. Le Tigre must get well."

The grandfather clock in the main hall bonged nine a.m. The cook busied herself scrubbing and washing the kitchen. The Noir kids were away at school, "Now I can get my work done. My, how those selfish brats mess up this place in their wild raids for snacks at night." She hid some fruit and cereal to smuggle home for her kids.

Madame Noir lay swinging in her hammock on the back patio nursing a 'morning tea' of rum and Coke. She flipped through her latest stack of Paris Reviews, selecting gowns and jewelry for herself and her daughter, Beatrice. Her big list for her next flight to France was almost complete.

A cool breeze blew softly across her face. She planned to fly to Paris with Beatrice after the healing ceremony for Le Tigre. They would have the luxury of personal fittings and attend a fashion show.

André felt relieved at this 'quieting down' of the household. He plunged his scrub brush back into the bucket of soapy suds. "I need a break," he said, scratching his ribs.

He stood up and eyed the grand marble staircase. "I'm going to explore. Perhaps I'll find a way out of this prison," he thought.

He tiptoed up the stairs and eased past Tigre's bedroom door. Two doors confronted him at the end of the long hall, each entrance bordered by mahogany, black with gold trim. Above the door on the right, inscribed in silver letters, were the words "This Noir Family Temple is dedicated to Legba."

A key dangled in the door. He smiled as he turned the key and slipped through the entrance.

Inside he marveled at the mysterious surroundings. "What does it all mean?" he thought.

He gazed at a dimly lit candle flickering next to a bone-handled silver machete knife. Shadows danced on a cat's skull. A bowl of shriveling fruit adorned a table on the left. A large wall hanging of strange symbols, animals, and trees dominated the scene. Rays of sunlight from a small skylight vibrated and danced on the altar.

André ventured into a small side room. Drums of different sizes lay disarranged in the corner. Headdresses, gowns, and ceremonial regalia hung on the wall. Sticks knobbed with carved skulls were on the floor.

He had never seen anything like this in his life. A double-door opened into a large main room. It resembled a dance floor he and his dad observed in a hotel in Jeremie, only it was much, much larger.

André stood in the richest voodoo temple in all of Haiti. Madame Noir denied nothing from the loas. "Here the voodoo loas are rich and powerful," he thought. "Why do they have to murder Hoot to make Le Tigre well? My Jesus wouldn't like that!"

The Noir temple complex included a large room where worshipers whirled into their final trances and fell to the floor completely exhausted.

Hypnotized by his strange surroundings, time stood still for André.

André suddenly heard voices, and hurried footsteps approaching. Madame Noir and her voodoo Priestess, Moogami, were inspecting the temple and preparing the ceremony. The Temple door slowly opened. André darted through a narrow side entrance marked "High Priestess Mambo Room."

André dripped with sweat. His heart pounded. "If I'm caught, they'll kill me," he thought.

Near a changing room/toilet, he found a secret stairway that led to the led to the ground floor. "Now I know a new way to get out of here," he mumbled breathlessly as he fled down the stairs, three steps at a time.

He raced back to his cleaning bucket and brush, and continued to clean the floor.

Their inspection completed, Madame bid the priestess Moogami farewell. "Don't be late. See you a week from today. I'll pay you then for the other half of the ceremony. Let's pray for a cloudless moonlight sky." And they kissed goodbye, pecking each others cheeks insincerely.

Madame turned toward André. Armed with her correction stick, she demanded, "Where were you, Restavec? You are never to leave your work until finished."

She whipped André unmercifully. Each blow

cut into his back. Bleeding, André yearned for pity and understanding. His moans fell on deaf ears. If he called out for help she might call for Dom, who specialized in pistol-whipping.

And then there was Jabou, Madame's youngest brother, who was a police captain. André remembered the fate of Émile, who was caned to death.

Madame marched out, tromping like a ruthless dictator.

André thanked God he wasn't discovered in the Temple. Madame Noir could have beaten him to death. He knew now where his little friend would die and who would kill him.

He finished mopping the floor. He fed and watered the hutia. "We'll soon be out of here, Hoot," he said.

He frowned as he imagined the wild beating of drums suddenly stopping to signal the sacrifice. He recalled the razor-sharp machete gleaming on the candle-lit altar.

…

Moogami returned to her husband, Marcel. "We're all set for Saturday night at the Noirs!" she cooed. "Her private temple is something else. Her Catholic priest would faint if he knew the truth about her."

Marcel, her voodoo husband priest, looked up from his cash box. As a successful priest, he normally took cash for his services, but occasionally he would receive a pig or a chicken. His business was very good, particularly his black magic, damning culprits behind the curses with higher loa power.

He exchanged phone calls and letters with his cousin, Alexandre, who practiced a form of voodoo in West Africa. Alexandre became financially successful as a bokor-sorcerer, accepting cases such as a Haitian in England bewitched by a jealous uncle in Nigeria.

Alexandre recently visited him and took part in several ceremonies and received consultant fees. Marcel's clients were very impressed.

Marcel took a deep breath. "My beloved Moogami, what if we delayed Le Tigre's ceremony for a month?"

"We can't do that. The Noirs are desperate. Look at the plans they've made. The money they've spent. The dozens invited. And finally, I don't believe our little sacrifice can last much longer."

"Well, it's just a thought. Keep it in mind. I just had a wild plan to turn our work for the Noirs into an even greater 'cash cow'."

"You're being silly, my darling," Moogami retorted.

Marcel smiled. "No, I'm being religious, dear. Each U.S. bank note is printed 'In God We Trust'."

"True, sweetie. But 'God' has a different meaning for you and me than for Christians in Haiti. Right?"

"Yes...dear." He glanced at his Rolex. "It's time to attend our local voodoo planning committee."

What is a Dirt Cookie?

A Haitian mud pie made of dirt, salt, water and vegetable shortening. It is a desperate way to feed a starving child.

Children eat these because they are all the family can afford. Food is often unavailable.

The "dirt cookie" presents a serious health problem because of parasites in the soil. These cause horrible illnesses and even death. A full tummy of baked dirt is no answer to starvation and disease.

15

The "Day" with Jabou

The next day Jabou stopped by the Noir mansion unexpectedly. "My dear sister, I need your help. One of my prisoners fell under the wheels of our jail cart which crushed his leg. I must replace him. I've got to move a load of cement blocks across town. We're building another 'holding facility'."

"How can I help you?" Madame handed him a mug of steaming coffee.

"I want to borrow your restavec all day tomorrow. I'll pay you ten dollars."

"No need." Madame answered. "Tigre and I owe you a favor. The restavec can go. I'll have the cook's daughter do his work."

Jabou took a long sip. "Now that we've settled on the restavec for tomorrow, I have a question that bothers me."

Madame Noir leaned forward. "Yes and what's that?"

Jabou sat back, his hands behind his neck.

"You've got tons of dollars, sis. You're filthy rich. Why not hire servants instead of having a restavec work for you?"

"I've got a cook."

"Get serious, dear sister. You know perfectly well what I mean."

Madame Noir folded her hands defiantly across her chest and said, "You and I each had a restavec as we grew up. We never cleaned up our messes. Our family paid for them. They were our property. We controlled them night and day. You specialized in girls and I, the boys. Don't forget that!"

"So what are you trying to tell me?" Jabou inquired.

"They fill a very personal need for me which a servant can't. I control their actions 24 hours a day."

Jabou reflected. "I remember, sis, when our mother died and our father sent us to school in New York to our exclusive Brooklyn high school."

Madame tongued her upper lip. "I was thirteen. It was a bad year."

"You brought your history book home and shared it with me showing me photos of Jewish men and women and children murdered in World War Two by the Nazis."

"Well brother, they should never have been born and Hitler was eliminating them when America, England, and France interrupted him."

"You hate people, don't you?"

"Some." Madame looked away vacantly.

"Men and boys, especially," she said.

"Why do you say that? Is it because *what* our Uncle Jacque did to you when he visited us shortly before we went to New York?"

"How did you know that?"

"I heard our father order him from the house. He threatened to kill him."

Madame Noir ranted on. "After all, Jabou, when all is said and done about restavecs, remember my dear brother that this has been our national tradition in Haiti for over 200 years. Back to the time we became free from our French masters."

"Well, come to the point, sis." Jabou remarked.

"So we should have the right to become slave owners ourselves," she answered.

"Well, sis, you've answered my question," Jabou said. "Have the restavec ready at sunup. Okay? Gotta run. Mind if I take this coffee with me? I'll return the cup in the morning."

Madame kissed him lightly on both cheeks. "No problem," she said, and watched his police jeep screech away with siren screaming full blast.

The next day began as usual. André had been working since five a.m. carrying water and preparing a fire to heat Madame's coffee. He wolfed down scraps of chicken and rice left by the Noir children from last night. André thought, "It's dirty and cold, but it's breakfast."

His tee shirt and shorts were wet. He had washed them last night in cold water. They were shredded, ripped and faded. But they were all he had to wear. He had no shoes. They were burned the night his mother and sister died.

The soiled, worn-out clothes Madame provided him remained hanging in the supply closet. André planned to use them when he escaped.

The next day, an early morning smog from charcoal fires invaded the slums of Port-au-Prince. The Noir mansion loomed high in Pétionville above the squalor, enjoying a cool breeze.

André fed and watered Hoot. No longer did Hoot curl up in the corner of his cage when André approached. He came to André. They had bonded.

André trusted the cook's daughter. She treated him with kindness and respect. He felt certain she would do the same for his little friend while he was away with Jabou. She would arrive with her mother, the cook, and serve Madame Noir's whims when her mother was occupied with other chores.

Jabou arrived late. "Jeep held up by traffic," he muttered. He shoved André in the back seat, next to his prisoner in red overalls. A man in his early twenties, but looked to be fifty.

Jabou dressed certain select prisoners in red. He said they were high risk. And, he added, " I can shoot them more easily if they try to escape."

Madame Noir waddled to the gate to see them off. Nodding towards André, she sipped her black coffee. "It's yours, brother, till midnight, if it can last that long. Goodbye."

Jabou plunged his car into the early morning chaos. The streets swelled rapidly. People begging, searching for work, and selling anything they could. A pack of stray dogs darted in front of them. Jabou leaned on the horn, blasting ahead through the crowds. He narrowly missed children chasing fruit spilled from a motorbike. A United Nations truck muscled into the stream of traffic.

Jabou stopped at his police station. A cart heavily loaded with concrete blocks parked in front.

A tall, barefoot man in front of the cart sipped water and wiped his face. Jabou had hired him for two dollars for ten hours per day to hand-pull this cart to and from the new police facility site. André remembered his father saying that such hard work would kill or maim a man after two years of such grueling labor.

"Everybody out!" yelled Jabou. "Attention! Listen up! You are to push this load to our new police site about a half mile away."

He gestured toward the tall man. "This man will guide you and help pull. You push. My plan is to move three loads today. There's water and some food in the cart for you. Protect it. Or you'll go hungry. Let's go!"

Pulling and pushing the cart was back-breaking. The tall man tugged and guided while André and the prisoner pushed. The cart's wheels needed grease. The tires were threadbare. Struggling through dense crowds, André kept his eyes on the food and water hidden among the cement blocks.

Occasionally André's companion would steal some fruit from a vendor's stand and share it with him. A kind lady on a mission bus tossed him a bread roll. It was squashed under a bus. A mongrel dog choked it down. The woman shrugged, "I'm so sorry."

Two hours passed. They threaded the cart to the construction site. There the unloading began. Jabou rushed ahead in his jeep to enjoy a long coffee with police friends as he waited for their arrival.

He looked menacingly at André and the prisoner, ordering them to unload and stack the blocks quickly.

As he tried to maintain his balance, André stepped on a broken bottle. A minor cut. It hurt. He could tolerate it more than the lash of Jabou's whip.

He remained quiet about the injury. The bleeding stopped. The throbbing pain continued. He hoped the cook would clean and treat it in the morning.

On the third return trip from the building site, André glimpsed a familiar face stepping off a yellow mission bus in the distance. His heart pounded. It was Headmaster Thompson. But André was too far away to get Thompson's attention. If he screamed, Jabou could beat him senseless. He couldn't take that chance. He must remain alive to return Hoot to Macaya. He asked himself, "Why is Mr. Thompson here? Is he searching for me?" Dejected, he resumed his slow trek back to Jabou's police station,

Thompson had tracked André past Les Cayes to the fishing village and boarded a boat for Jacmel. In Jacmel, he was told by a cab driver about the group's Pétionville destination.

"André's probably living with wealthy criminals," he concluded. "But where? He must be desperate."

Jabou returned André to the Noir mansion around midnight. Madame had gone to bed. André felt exhausted but blessed on his bed of rags. He now knew places to hide and roads to follow for his escape to freedom.

Do Haitians have electricity and running water in their homes?

No, most living quarters are extremely simple. Some homes in major cities are wired for electricity, but may only receive power a few hours a day. Homes in the villages are usually lighted by candles. Since batteries are expensive, flashlights are a luxury.

Without running water in their homes, many children in Haiti are sent every day to fetch water from a river or well, sometimes an hour away. Many children then have to carry on their heads a water container filled with 25 pounds of water back to their homes each morning.

Pure drinking water is precious and expensive. Many children die each year from infectious diseases caused from drinking unpurified water.

16

Madame Noir's Mistake

Madame Noir sank into a large bean bag cushion. Tigre stretched out on his imported La-Z-Boy chair. From their large picture window they gazed below at the huddled shacks.

They enjoyed their feeling of power and separation from the masses below.

Madame fanned herself furiously. "The air conditioners aren't working too well, dear. We need to replace them. I want our believers to be comfortable as we contact the spirits of the dead and the loa this weekend. We may have to replace several window units."

Tigre nodded, "Do what you have to do, my dear. Money's no problem." He winked and looked up. He patted his tankard of rum, which he called 'his morning tea.' It dulled his mind and his pain. "By the way," he questioned, "can we keep our little sacrifice alive for the ceremony? I looked at it this morning. It's awfully puny."

"You worry too much, my dear husband. My friend in Santo Domingo told me we can get one from the Dominican Republic. The hutia there are protected by the Zoological Society of London and other groups. However, we should be able to steal one and smuggle it into Haiti for a price, of course."

Tigre shrugged. "But it's not the same, my dear. It must be from Mount Macaya. My ancestral spirit made that clear. I'm calling Dom to get some proper food for our little critter."

He punched the numbers on his cell. No response. Tigre didn't know that Dom was unavailable playing poker at the Crystal Palace.

Tigre sighed, "Just when I need him, he isn't around."

"Rest easy, Tigre. All is ready for the ceremony," Madame crowed. She took great pride in flaunting her wealth before her voodoo friends. She smiled. "What the Catholic Church can't do, my voodoo chapel can."

Tigre tried to breathe and lapsed into a hacking cough. He fell asleep, physically drained.

The front gate buzzer sounded. It was Jabou again, stopping for coffee. Madame Noir greeted him, "Please stay for the whole afternoon and keep Tigre company."

Jabou peered at Tigre. "He's asleep. He doesn't

need my company," Jabou replied.

"You never really told me what happened to my last restavec?" Madame asked.

"I told you he's with Jesus. He went hysterical at the police station. Out of control. Guess we beat him too hard. At least he died quickly. His real name was Émile something."

André entered the room just in time to hear the name, Émile. He thought about the note. "It really happened," he thought. He darted unseen into the kitchen.

Madame Noir sighed, "I must go now. I have an appointment with my Italian dressmaker. I must look my best for our guests on Saturday."

Jabou excused himself. "Got to run now and fill up the jail. We need all the free labor we can get."

André accomplished two important things as he kept up the pace of Madame Noir's relentless foolish whims.

First, he secretly dipped into her hidden stash of imported Swiss chocolates to cope with his lack of food and energy.

And secondly, he carefully observed Madame Noir's bedtime routine. She was a rum and coke addict at night. King-sized bottles of each were always on her bed stand. Every night she downed a stiff nightcap before fluffing her pillows. "She will be hopelessly drunk tonight," André thought.

During the day Madame Noir wore a brass ring of keys for the mansion gates and for her wall safe. At night she hung the keys close to her bed. She stowed a loaded revolver in her bed stand 'for emergencies.'

Friday arrived. "Tonight's the night." André prayed. "Please protect us, God."

That night Madame felt unusually tired. The week of preparations for tomorrow's voodoo event had worn her out. She doubled the rum in her nightcap. "I must sleep well tonight," she sighed.

Tigre kept guard dogs chained near his bed for extra security. André had begged the cook to quietly feed them an extra dose of Tigre's 'sleeping medicine.'

"Dear God, it's the one way I can help André," she prayed. "He needs all the help he can get. Jesus, keep him safe."

André lay awake. He heard Madame lock the gates, flush the toilet, and close her bedroom door. "She was so tipsy she forgot to lock her bedroom door," André thought. "What luck!"

Her Louis the Fourteenth clock rang the midnight hour. "Time to go," André said to himself. He pulled out Émile's note with his mother's cross necklace from its hole and put it in a safe place in his pocket.

He quietly tip-toed into Madame Noir's bedroom, lifted the keys from the wall and returned to his closet. He arranged the clothes he had never worn to resemble his body asleep. He loaded plastic bottles of water, scraps of fruit and chicken into a sack.

Arriving at Hoot's cage, he whispered, "No sound now, my little friend." He nestled Hoot into a sling.

Reaching the back gate, André accidentally dropped the keys. His heart raced. A rat scurried across the alley. He froze. No further sound. He retrieved the keys and unlocked the back gate. Once in the alley, he locked the gate from the outside, and hurled the keys into a drainage ditch.

Keeping within the back alleys and service roads, André crept quietly in the shadows down to the nearest main road to Port-au-Prince. Suddenly, a police van careened into view, its searchlight madly swaying. André dived for cover behind a pile of trash. The van sped by them toward the back gate of the Noir mansion.

"Sorry, Hoot. I didn't mean to crush you!" he apologized. With his knee skinned and pant leg torn, he looked at Hoot. "Once they're out of sight we'll head for the main road."

How does HIV/ AIDS affect Haiti and the children there?

HIV is a virus which if left untreated can lead to AIDS -- Acquired Immune Deficiency Syndrome.

AIDS results in the human body shutting down its ability to protect itself from disease and leads to early death. AIDS is spread through infected blood transfusions or through sexual contact with an infected person.

The number of people living with HIV/AIDS in Haiti is around 150,000 with the highest prevalence among women.

Transmission of the virus from a mother to her child during childbirth or nursing can occur and many of Haiti's children are directly impacted due to a sick parent.

17

On The Run

The night patrol police jeep screeched to a stop. Its front mounted lights lit up the alley like a Hollywood opening night. Three armed men jumped out and checked Tigre's back gate. "All locked. No problem." The driver revved the engine and shot off into the blackness.

Tigre had hired local police to inspect his gates every midnight. It was an extra expense. He said it was worth it. He had many enemies. He bragged how Dom had gunned down a hit man who climbed the mansion wall into Tigre's room last year.

In the valley below, André held Hoot close, taking refuge behind a rock pile. He kept to the side streets and narrow lanes, always in the shadows.

He planned to reach the main highway west of Porte Au Prince and head to Miragoâne where he hoped to find Émile's uncle Vincent. Hopefully, Vincent would help him and Hoot return to Macaya.

At night, the streets of Port-au-Prince became

empty for fear of zombies who do evil under control of a bokor and fear of loagaroo monsters who are in league with the devil, searching for human blood every night.

André wasn't worried about the zombies and loagaroo. He was afraid of the human monsters who would soon awaken.

Dawn was several hours away. André imagined the fury and anger of Tigre and Madame when they discovered he and Hoot were missing. He shuddered as he contemplated their fate, if they found them.

Ahead lay a police checkpoint. Beyond it was a bridge spanning a wide drainage ditch. A guard slept inside a small building. Another sentry lay prone, his AK scoped rifle across his chest, his finger on the trigger. André prayed. "Thank you, Lord. They're asleep."

André whispered to Hoot, "Don't make a sound." He undressed down to his underwear, rolled his tee shirt and tucked them into the sling with Hoot and their meager food supply. He lifted the heavy bundle on his head, and slowly waded through the putrid water to the other side. Sometimes the river slime reached just below his neck.

Half way across he froze. One guard woke up to relieve himself on the street. André waited until all was quiet again. His arms were killing him as he steadied the precious load on his head. "So close, my little friend," he warned.

"We'll spend the night under the bridge ahead." Wading to a safe place out of sight from the sentries, he laid his heavy load gently on the bank, shadowed from the street lights and dressed.

He and Hoot shared clean water from a plastic bottle. He sponged his body clean as best he could with the night air slowly drying him and then dressed. Hoot dozed in André's arms. André counted his little friend's heartbeats and fell asleep. For the moment, Madame Noir was out of his mind.

Why do Haitian tombs have alcoves (small openings)?

These are places reserved for food offerings to the ancestral spirits of deceased relatives. These edible gifts are given by the surviving relatives on special anniversaries.

18

Le Tigre's Final Roar

A foreboding silence pervaded the Noir household. It was Saturday, a full moon weekend. The mansion was spotless. Madame Noir had conducted her full inspection yesterday.

However, Madame's window air conditioners remained idle. The municipal power stations were empty. After two months without pay, the workers had abandoned their jobs. Madame overslept. Last night's excess of rum and the muggy room temperature plunged her into deep sleep.

Her bedside cell jangled "Happy Days Are Here Again!" Confused, she groped for the phone. She snapped off her sleeping mask and fumbled the phone to her ear. It was the cook. "I'm locked out, Madame. Please open the alley gate."

Madame frantically looked for her keys. "How could I be so forgetful?" she slurred. She scratched through the bed stand drawers. "Where are my emergency keys?" she screamed. She couldn't locate them.

Something else was terribly wrong. No coffee at her bedside. Rushing to the kitchen she saw the empty cage. A quick look in the supply closet revealed the awful truth. André and the hutia were gone.

Fright and rage consumed her as she raced from one room to another.

She phoned her brother, Jabou, to sound the alarm, offering a reward of $1000 U.S. dollars to anyone returning the restavec and the animal immediately. Jabou called his police staff to fan out and search the suburbs.

Only a few responded. It was Saturday. Most were gambling at a rooster fight.

The cook sat on a pile of rubble outside the back gate. She knew that André had fled. She prayed that he and the hutia were safe in their dash for freedom. Madame finally found an extra set of keys in her medicine cabinet. She unlocked the back alley gate and let the cook in. "Do you know anything about this?"

Enraged, she shook the cook.

"No, Madame. Nothing," the cook answered.

Her lips sealed. "This lie's for you, God. Forgive me."

Madame cried out for her children to help her. She found them sprawled asleep in front of their glaring TV. The weather report from Miami blared. She kicked them awake.

"Go find that bastard restavec!" She yelled. They scrambled to their bedrooms to laze away the weekend. Saturday classes for failing students had been canceled.

"They're impossible. They take after their father. They make me sick," she sneered.

Madame dashed into Tigre's upstairs master suite. Tigre was snoring, unaware of Madame's tragic discovery. She pounded him into a sitting position. "Wake up, you fool! You drink too much! The restavec and the animal are gone! Escaped!"

Tigre stuttered weakly, "W-W-What am I going to do now?"

Tigre staggered to his feet and slipped into his dressing gown. He stared into his full-length mirror, shocked by his reflection of hopelessness. Dazed. He mumbled, "The ceremony's tonight."

Sweating profusely, he buzzed the intercom for Couteau and Dom. "Come quickly. I need you, n-n-now," and his voice trailed off.

He wobbled out barefoot into the hall and stood before the marble stairs spiraling down two floors below to the chandeliered entry way. He clawed at his heart, unable to breathe. He tumbled head over heels, crashing step-by-step to rest at the feet of

Couteau and Dom, who had rushed to meet him.

"Oh my God, he's dead!" Dom cried, feeling Tigre's pulse. "His neck appears to be broken."

Couteau added. "This changes everything."

Madame Noir arrived breathless and faint. "I couldn't reach him in time. I feel terrible." The three stared at Tigre's lifeless body.

Madame sat on the entrance bench, shaken. Her voice squeaked. "Get me a drink."

Regaining her composure, Madame now had a funeral to prepare. "Call our Catholic priest. Clean up Tigre's body. I swear that I will personally kill the restavec and the animal."

She called Moogami, her priestess, immediately to tell her about this sudden tragedy. Moogami, shocked by Tigre's death, exclaimed, "Madame, this changes everything. Your life is now in grave danger. I must see you immediately after you bury your husband. I will call you."

Madame, dazed, clicked off and dropped her cell to the floor. "What does she mean?" she asked herself.

The Catholic priest administered the last rites over Tigre's body laid out in the mansion foyer. He retired with Madame Noir for a toast to her late husband and scheduled the date for his funeral mass.

Black curtains draped the Noir mansion. Madame openly displayed her sadness. She wore solid black and drank from a black mug.

Madame would be preoccupied for the next few days with her husband's burial place, monument, and many legal matters involving the will. "Got to keep my money hungry brats out of the wall safe," she thought.

Madame Noir quickly discovered Jabou was her most dependable ally in pursuing the restavec and the hutia. Jabou hoped to inherit the Noir godfather status and share much of the wealth with his sister.

Jabou greeted his sister shortly after receiving the news that Tigre had died. He embraced Madame tightly. "I'm so sorry, Mauvette." He called her by her first name, thinking that he would sound more like family who deeply cared.

"Never call me Mauvette again," Madame warned. "Call me 'sis.' 'Mauvette' is too close to 'Mauvaise,' which means bad. Our mother called me 'Mauvette' and I hate it.

"I must prepare for Tigre's mass. Get the restavec and hutia with whatever it takes. Call me the moment you capture them."

"Like I was going to say, Sis, when we catch the restavec, I'll have a correction session with it at the police station. You can be assured he will promptly see the grave faster than that Émile kid."

"And I'll be there to help you do the job, too," Madame replied. "By the way, how are Dom and Couteau assisting in all of this?"

Jabou answered, "They have contacted Tigre's 'business associates' to help locate the animal and Restavec.

"In fact, they are questioning many around Pétionville who might have seen something."

Dom and Couteau met for drinks at the Crystal Palace Dance Hall and Bar in the tourist district. They had interviewed everyone who had entered the Tigre mansion since the hutia and Restavec arrived.

"What about the cook?" Couteau asked.

"She's clean. Has a houseful of kids to feed plus six others from up country, all looking for work."

"What about our guards?"

"They all live in the front gate barracks. Very loyal. Want to keep their jobs. Many mouths to feed."

Couteau leaned closer. "You and I both know that we have more important things to do other than get that restavec and hutia. I'm looking into ways we can cut into Tigre's fortune and bankroll a gang. He's underpaid us for years. As soon as the restavec thing blows over, we'll talk about it more."

"Back to work now." Dom winked. "Crime is one sure steady job to keep food on the table. Let's go pick out some classy duds for Tigre's funeral."

They climbed into the Rav-4. Backing out, the power brakes failed. Dom now had to depend on the hand brake to stop.

Dom winked at Couteau. "What do you say to trading this Rav for a more expensive car like a Mercedes? We'll use Tigre's cash and attend his mass in style!" He waved Tigre's credit card.

Couteau laughed. "Sounds great. Let's go! New car! New suit! Wow!"

When will child slavery end in Haiti?

Child slavery will end when Haiti's citizens recognize the restavec system as evil, cease to tolerate it, and hold those involved accountable. Haitian Christian educators, ministers, and community leaders are even now working to train the next generation to value each person's worth in God's sight.

19

On the Road
to Miragoâne

André and Hoot slept little under the bridge. Traffic rattled above through the night. The guards were now placed on high alert. Madame's publicized reward sweetened their cooperation. They were determined to snare the pair.

Canal slime itched all over André's body. "I'd give anything for a nice warm shower," he whispered. "My sponge-bath didn't get me clean."

"You must be thirsty." André opened another bottle of water and rationed gulps into Hoot's mouth.

"Time to go, my little friend, while it's still dark." André slowly staggered around piles of flood debris - mildewed paper, wood scraps, wet limbs, and garbage saturated with dirty water.

He slowly climbed the slippery slope and silently merged into a procession of early morning workers going to their jobs. Others were trying to beat the stream of cars, trucks and carts which congested the roads at daylight.

André glanced back. He hadn't been noticed by the bridge sentries. They were asleep in their jeeps. "So far, so good," He thought.

Ahead a major jam of trucks, tap-taps and motor bikes froze traffic to a standstill. André saw a sign at the intersection marked "Highway No. 2, turn left, Miragoâne 83 kilometers."

A bus carrying voodoo pilgrims to Bassin Bleu's sacred waterfalls had been hit by a black limo. People swarmed around waiting for the police to unravel the mess. A tow truck and pickup with cables sat idle nearby waiting to provide service for a fee.

André edged closer around the impasse of vehicles. Pedestrians were getting through where cars rolled slowly west. That was the direction he wanted to go.

A large truck parked by the side of the road stood packed with boxes of fruit, clothing and building materials. Its cab door advertised the company, Vincent Lavalier and Sons - General Merchants - Miragoâne.

"Could that be Émile's Uncle?" he asked himself. Hoot's ears perked up – sensing André's excitement and relief. André broke into a trot toward the truck. Hoot, nestled in his sling, bounced with every step.

André slowly approached the Lavalier transport truck. The driver was on his knees inspecting the tires. He thumped his spare and looked at André. "Back off, kid. You're too close. No hitchhiking or I'll whack you." Scared, Hoot ducked his head back into the sling.

André stopped. He held high Émile's note and cross necklace. "I have a message for Monsieur Lavalier," he pleaded. "It's from his nephew, Émile."

"Give it to me." The driver studied the note. He was visibly moved by the tiny cross and Émile's note about his impending death. He looked André up and down. "You've been through hell, haven't you?"

André stumbled, "Y-Y-Yes, monsieur."

"I've got a son about your age. You can climb aboard the truck with your little animal. Your job will be to keep the tarps tied down securely. Let me know when anyone messes with our load."

"Thank you, I will," André answered.

The driver smiled. "I'll take you to Miragoâne to see my boss, Vincent. However, if I'm stopped by the police I'll tell them you're my nephew."

He continued, "I'll put some food and water near the tail gate. We won't be stopping for a long while. Bon appétit."

The driver locked himself into the cab of the truck. He stowed his emergency pistol under some delivery documents, and started the engine. He instantly shifted into low gear and pressed a radio station button on the dash. Surrounded by the steady beat of Haitian Reggae, he maneuvered his loaded truck into the snail-paced traffic.

His cargo was boxes of surplus canned vegetables for sale in stores catering to the poor in coastal areas in and around Miragoâne. Some were people who were turned back by the U.S. Coast Guard years ago when they tried to seek asylum in the U.S.

At La Salle, an eastbound Lavalier truck stood parked. The driver honked and motioned for André's truck to pull over.

"You must detour north at the next turn," its driver said. "You'll reach Miragoâne safely that way. I narrowly escaped four armed thugs searching every vehicle. I rammed through their blockade of rocks. They shot out my front windshield. One of the thugs has red hair."

André overheard the warning. "That's got to be Couteau," he thought. He held Hoot closer.

The driver, a devout Catholic, crossed himself. "We could have been killed had we continued on that road. Thank you, God." He glanced at André. "It's okay, kid. We'll be delayed for a couple of hours." He swerved the truck onto the detour road.

André marveled at the coastal scenery. The rugged Rock Point. The blue-green sea. The crowded villages. People laughing. Children playing "futbol" (soccer) with duct-taped paper balls. Their games were interrupted by wandering goats and chickens, and by trucks passing through.

It was refreshing to see so many happy people, creating fun and laughter with little but love for one another. "So different from Madame Noir in her house of hate," he thought.

Is there corruption in Haiti?

Corruption can be defined as "abusing entrusted power to gain personal benefits." In 2013, Haiti and ranked 163rd ("highly corrupt") out of 177 countries. (Transparency International's Corruption Peception Index)

Until Haiti has an empowered workforce which is trained to follow Biblical standards of honesty and integrity, corruption will continue. Christian schools and churches are dedicated to achieving this through training Haiti's future leaders in ethical standards as found in Christ's teachings.

20

Grandmother's Spirit Raves

The Noir mansion remained in an uproar. Tigre's Mass had been held. His body had been laid to rest in an elegant stone tomb. The restavec and hutia had escaped. Madame's teenagers were going wild.

Madame's cell phone played "Happy Days are Here Again!" – a catchy tune that rarely epitomized her life now. She looked frazzled as she clopped across the patio to pick up her phone. "What next?" She screamed at the ceiling.

"It's Moogami, your priestess," a voice said. "Jabou phoned me to cancel tonight's ceremony."

"He beat me to it. I was going to call you just now," Madame Noir answered.

"We've got serious problems, Madame. I must see you at once. This cannot wait. I'm on my way to see you now."

Madame Noir tried to delay her. She was too late. Moogami had hung up.

Two hours passed. Moogami honked in front

of Madame's gates. Madame Noir checked the security monitor. "It's okay. Let her enter."

"No coffee for me. I must sit down," Moogami said, breathless, fanning herself.

"Madame, as I said earlier, we've got serious problems!"

"Like what?" Madame cocked her head.

"To begin, my relative who stole the hutia from Macaya has been arrested. He needs money for a lawyer and to get released from jail."

"Well?" Madame replied.

"You haven't paid me, Madame. I need to send him money right now!" Moogami said.

"Also…" Moogami continued, "The spirit of Angeline has contacted me. She's livid. She's been denied her hutia blood – the cosmic food you promised her. She's famished. Her spirit now demands to consume the restavec's blood."

"But I don't have the restavec."

"You were careless. You let it slip away. If no restavec, you will suffer her curse."

"Such as…"

"Dying from AIDS. She will make sure you become infected before the next full moon."

"You're kidding!"

"No. Remember that you slept with him as his wife."

Madame coughed uncontrollably. "What am I to do?"

Moogami looked at her straight in the eyes. "Get the restavec immediately."

Moogami inspected her new black fingernails. "On second thought, there may be another solution."

"What's that?" Madame's eyes opened wide with hope.

"My husband, Sébastien, assists me in all my voodoo rites. He's a priest with special knowledge of powerful medicines. You need to see him," Moogami advised.

"How much is this going to cost me?" Madame fanned herself like a cornered hummingbird.

"Counting your expenses already, plus his services, only $25,000 dollars U.S."

"$25,000!" Madame's head bulged to the bursting point. "That's robbery!" She hissed, clenching her teeth.

"It's up to you whether you want to live and avoid a horrible death."

Madame Noir wrung her hands. She stiffened into stoic shock. She looked as if she were possessed by a zombie.

Madame Noir took fifteen minutes to regain her composure. She strained to stand. "I'll be back in a minute. Wait here." She shuffled to her wall safe, counted out twenty-five $1000 US notes and marched back into the room.

She slapped the money in Moogami's lap. "This should do it for now. Get that evil spirit off my back."

"There's one more thing, Madame. You must add another $10,000. I only accept payment in advance now."

"What's the $10,000 for?" Madame Noir asked astonished.

Moogami replied, "We're going into black magic. Sorcery is a better word for it. To totally eliminate the deceased Grandmother's curse, we will need to enter her tomb and take pieces of her bones. This can be done, but will take time and money. We've got people to help us. And they need to be paid."

Madame Noir realized she couldn't win. Voodoo was a costly religion. She retrieved $10,000 more and dropped it on the floor. Moogami scooped it up. "I'll be back in touch with you tomorrow."

What is the name of the money used in Haiti?

The official currency of Haiti is the Haitian Gourde ("gude"). In 2013, a U.S. dollar was worth 42 Haitian Gourdes. Many businesses also accept U.S. money, but will only accept bills which have no rips or tears in them, due to the fear of accepting counterfeit U.S. currency.

21

Uncle Vincent

The Lavalier truck pulled into the Miragoâne wharf parking lot. Yard lights flared on. Vincent Lavalier rushed to the truck. "Bienvenue, André." (Welcome, André). He kissed and hugged André.

André was puzzled. "How did you know my name?"

"Christophe, my driver, phoned me. What a wonderful surprise! Felicity, my wife, has supper ready. Let's go immediately to my home."

André hugged the driver and thanked him.

"We've a nice place for you and your pet. Needless to say, we're very happy to have you as our guest."

Lavalier asked the driver to stay for the evening meal. The driver declined the invitation. He needed to unload the cargo and his wife and kids were expecting him.

The sweet aroma of delicious food greeted André as he was ushered into the Lavalier kitchen. Felicity hugged and kissed him. He felt overwhelmed with love.

"We know you're hungry, André, and your little friend as well. But first, there's the lavatory, a shower and fresh clean clothes. And then, just as soon as you're ready, we'll eat."

A palette of blankets lay on the floor for Hoot, with a bowl of water and a pan of roots and fruit to nibble.

They all sat down at the table and bowed their heads. Lavalier said, "Let us pray and eat." They thanked God for André's and the hutia's safe arrival.

"I talked with your father and Mr. Thompson and Pierre Fontaine about your being here with us. They are overjoyed that you are here as our guest."

After the meal, André presented Émile's note and the necklace to the Lavaliers. "We'll treasure Émile's note and my sister's necklace forever," Lavalier said. " I will frame them to hang in our family's prayer room."

Lavalier excused himself from the dining room. He returned shortly with a photo of Émile as a young child. "Here, take this, André. It's Émile. Though he never met you, I would like you to have it."

"Thank you," André replied.

"I talked to your father, and Mr. Thompson, and Pierre Fontaine. They are overjoyed.

"Émile's life was a nightmare." Lavalier

sobbed. "If only I had known, I could have rescued my nephew. You see, his mother, my sister, sold Émile to the Noirs when her husband died and left her destitute. Émile was 10." He trembled as he spoke. Felicity softly massaged his back.

"Let's phone your father now, André." He punched in the number. "He's at Camp Perrin, waiting for you. You'll see him tomorrow. The Fontaines are flying in by helicopter to pick you up in the morning." Handing André his cell phone, Lavalier said "You must talk to your father. He's on the phone now,".

André and his father, Henri, talked for an hour. André painfully described his ordeal as a slave. Henri detailed the funeral of his wife and daughter.

The conversation ended with André saying, "I'll see you soon. I love you, dad. Au revoir, goodbye for now."

In a few hours, they would be hugging one another. Tonight would be a sleepless blur. Tomorrow, a new life.

What do children eat and what type of clothing do they wear in Haiti?

The most common food that children eat is Haitian beans and rice, flavored with a Haitian mushroom called "djon-djon". Many only get to have meat mixed in their meals occasionally – usually a small piece of fish, chicken, or goat. Locally grown Haitian fruit such as bananas, plantains, mangos, and papaya are also served during mealtime. Children also eat various porridges made of squash, millet, plantains, or okra combined with cornmeal or flour and usually with sugar.

School children are required to wear a uniform. After school or on weekends, most wear secondhand clothing which comes from donations from other countries. On Sundays, Christian parents in Haiti try to dress their children to look the best they possibly can, out of respect for God (Bondye).

22

Macaya Again

The Lavaliers drove André, cradling the hutia, to the helicopter landing spot. They promised they would visit him later at Sunshine Academy's annual festival of music, drama, and dance.

"André, you must gain weight and get lots of sleep," Felicity Lavalier smiled. "We love you so much."

"Thank you again for Émile's note and my sister's necklace." Vincent Lavalier blinked back tears.

They watched the "Save Macaya" helicopter circle, hover and gently land at Miragoâne airfield.

Pierre Fontaine piloted the craft. He had flown for the Canadian Air Force in his early twenties. He stored the copter at Camp Perrin. "One of the big perks of my job," he said, "is flying this baby." He lifted off with Marie toward Miragoâne.

Above the roar of the copter blades he leaned toward his wife Marie, "I know you're concerned about the expense of this trip."

"By air it's safer and quicker," Pierre said to

Marie. "We have a precious cargo of two who need protection, food and medical care. We can't take any chances of breaking down on the road. Besides, our home office will understand."

Vincent Lavalier invited the Fontaines to stay for lunch. "Thank you, monsieur, but we must return as quickly as possible. André's father is anxiously waiting for us at Camp Perrin. And we must drive to our research station this afternoon."

The Fontaines thanked the Lavaliers for their compassionate care of André and the hutia. "We are forever grateful," Marie said.

André gave the Lavaliers kisses and a loving hug without speaking.

"That's okay, André. You need to board now," Vincent said.

The helicopter roared its propellers and whirred upward to a comfortable altitude, above Mont Solognac. Thirty minutes later the pilot nudged André. He shouted above the pulsating noise of the blades, "We've a special surprise for you before we land. Look down!"

He circled the Saint Mathurin waterfall below.

Voodoo believers waved as they waded and bathed in the sacred waters. Many knew the Fontaines as friends and waved back.

The Camp Perrin landing field lay quiet. It

was midday siesta time. The wind sock hung limp. The helicopter rocked down into the vacant passenger area.

The Thompsons pulled up. Henri, André's father, jumped out of their car and ran with open arms toward the helicopter.

The Fontaines lowered André to the runway. Marie cuddled the hutia.

Henri swept André into his arms. "Welcome home, son. You're safe now."

The walked slowly arm-in-arm toward Thompson's car.

Marie gathered them together for a moment. "I've made reservations for all of you to stay tonight at the Le Recul Hotel. You are guests of the Save Macaya Association.

"After a cool drink at the hotel let's all go up the mountain for Hoot's reunion with his parents."

"Amen to that!" echoed Pierre. "It'll be a mountain top experience!" He laughed.

After a tiring trip of winding roads and hairpin turns they arrived at the Mount Macaya Research Center.

"We'll go inside in a moment," Marie said. "I phoned ahead for our housekeeper, Bernadette, to make tea."

"But first, let's get Hoot to his family." They

all trooped behind Marie, snuggling the little animal, to the caged enclosure a short distance down the mountain. The four hutias inside scurried restlessly about as they approached.

"I believe they've picked up the scent." Marie said, as she placed Hoot to a small entry gate and scooted him in.

Hoot was quickly nosed by his parents. They frolicked excitedly. "You're home, little one!" exclaimed Marie. "Okay, let's go and let them have their family reunion alone."

They returned to the Fontaine kitchen. "Nothing like home sweet home," said Marie, as Bernadette poured the tea.

"Oh, by the way, let's tune in the news and see if our latest news is being telecast. We did call TV stations in Port-au-Prince that the hutia had been found."

Pierre clicked on the TV to listen to the latest news from Port-au-Prince.

Death notices and funeral dates were announced including Tigre Noir's. A voice interrupted. "This news bulletin just in. The Mount Macaya hutia has been found. Lab assistant arrested. Bail denied."

"Let's drink to that!" Thompson raised his cup of tea.

"We'll convict that thief." Pierre Fontaine said. "The felon's confessed."

Another bulletin flashed: "Two die in attempted robbery. Dominique Lasalle and Couteau Bonaparte were shot dead east of Léogâne on Highway 2. Their three accomplices were arrested and now face charges in Port-au-Prince." André gasped as their mug shots popped up on the screen.

After tea, André returned to the caged sanctuary to watch Hoot cavorting around some distance away. He shouted, "Good-bye for now. I'll see you again tomorrow, I promise. Remember, I love you." Hoot chomped undisturbed on a bowl of tasty roots.

The Thompsons, André, and his father returned to the Le Recule Hotel for the night.

Why are waterfalls important in Haiti?

They are believed to be sacred. One example is the falls at Villa-Bonheur near Mirabalais about two and a half hours' drive from Port-au-Prince.

Each year on July 16, thousands bathe in its pools. It is Haiti's biggest voodoo pilgrimage to a waterfall.

Haitians appreciate tourists who show respect when visiting their religious sites.

23

The Celebration

Today was the day for André to return home. His prayers had been answered.

His room at the Le Recule Hotel was very comfortable, but he barely slept since he was too excited to relax.

André bounced out of bed. He took a long shower and dressed into his new clothes his dad had brought for him. They smelled good. He felt clean. Admiring himself in the mirror, he smiled, "God is good!"

Henri and André enjoyed breakfast privately in their room. It was their first time together alone to catch up on all the news. The conversation turned somber as Henri related again the details of the funeral and the graveside services for André's mother and sister.

Thompson knocked at their door. "It's time to drive you to the Sunshine Academy. We should be there in about an hour," Thompson announced.

His Ford four-wheeler lurched and groaned through the mountain hills and valleys. "This old car needs medical attention." Thompson laughed. "It's suffering from auto-ritis."

Mrs. Thompson sighed. "He's on a humor roll. Ignore him."

They passed a voodoo shrine, the last major landmark before the school grounds came into view.

"Do you remember this road, André? We widened and paved it while you were gone," Mr. Thompson said.

The school's assembly hall loomed into view. "Tomorrow, the students will welcome you home, André. Della and I have prepared rooms for you and your father in our home for tonight. You may stay longer if you wish. Snacks are laid out in the kitchen and Della will warm up food you desire."

André slept soundly until six o'clock the next day. He had survived with little food and impure water for weeks. He had never been so hungry and tired.

The next morning, a welcome banner "Bi-envenue, André" fluttered above the entrance to Sunshine Academy. Students waving school colors lined both sides of the road to the assembly hall.

The student president of André's class escorted André, Henri, and the Thompsons to the podium. The auditorium was packed. Students sat in the aisles and on the open window ledges.

The audience bowed in prayer, thanking God for André's safe return and closing with a resounding "Amen." The student choir sang their hearts out in Creole and French hymns to God.

The Thompson family dog, John Wesley, wandered in sniffing across the stage. Henri jumped up and led it to sit by André. The students laughed. The dog made the program fun.

André looked up, pleasantly surprised as Marie Fontaine carried Hoot, wearing a tiny school tee shirt, to sit in her lap. She said, "Sorry we're late. We had a flat tire."

Mr. Thompson announced, "We're honored you folks are here." He stood at the mike motioning the students to quiet down, then invited Henri to speak.

Henri gave a short summary about his son's disappearance and captivity as a slave child. He rejoiced that André was alive. The students clapped and whistled.

Marie Fontaine held up Hoot, the hutia. Thompson, André and the student class president declared Hoot to be Sunshine's new mascot. Hoot's tiny tee shirt was inscribed: "Sunshine's #1 Mascot".

Raising both hands to quiet the students, Pierre Fontaine took his turn at the mike. "It is my pleasure to present a distinguished award. As you know, the hutia is an endangered animal in Haiti. We can't afford to lose any more. They are a national resource unique to this country."

He continued. "André, please come forward. You saved the life of this precious animal. For your heroism, the Save Macaya Foundation presents you with a check for $1,000 U.S. dollars for your college fund. This is the reward money for whoever returned our lost hutia alive and you are that person."

André bowed and thanked the Save Macaya Foundation. The audience clapped loudly.

"I have another important announcement to make. A Certificate of Appreciation to André Arnaud from the Nature Preservation Committee of Haiti.

"Congratulations, André. Your father, Henri, will now present you with this award."

André put the check in his front shirt pocket and waved the Certificate. He beamed a big 'Thank You,' and hugged Henri and the Thompsons.

The assembly roared with applause then burst into song, "A'lam kontan, Jezi renmen mwen!" ("I'm so happy, Jesus loves me!")

André embraced dozens of his classmates and teachers. He smiled. "I'll see you tomorrow in class. I promise."

The Fontaines said, "It's time to get Hoot back

to his parents. Perhaps, André, you and your dad can visit us this weekend and you can feed Hoot and play with him."

Henri replied, "We can do that. Any chance of having a piece of your Canadian pineapple up-side-down cake?"

Marie yelled back, "I believe we can handle that. See you Saturday about noon! Bring your appetite and smiles!"

"And don't forget 'futbol' practice after you've recovered," said the school coach.

Henri smiled. "André, I've got another big surprise for you. Mr. Thompson will drive us there."

André soon stood at the very place where his house had been burned to the ground, but now it had been rebuilt and furnished. He entered his new bedroom, collapsed on his bed and fell asleep. He felt exhausted and blessed.

What do Haiti's children do in school?

They learn how to read and write and improve their basic communication skills in Creole and French. They study math and how to budget their money.

Children are encouraged to improve their health through exercise, drinking pure water and eating nutritious food.

Games, like futbol (soccer) and relay races are played to develop self-esteem, group co-operation and physical fitness.

The goal of education in Haiti is to help each child live a productive and happy life.

24

Fourteen Years Later

Fourteen years later, André was now the Headmaster of Sunshine Academy. Its enrollment had grown to 200 students with half a dozen more girls than boys. The majority were former restavecs or orphans found abandoned in Haiti's larger cities.

Thanks to a child sponsorship organization which matched each child to a sponsor in the U.S. or Canada, they were given full board and tuition scholarships.

André had received an International Christian Fund scholarship to further his schooling. He graduated at the top of his class at Columbia University in school administration with special training in religion and literacy. He continued his studies to receive a Ph.D. His thesis was titled: "Educating Haiti out of Poverty and Child Slavery."

Henri, his father said, "The world smiled on André, especially when André met his wife, Maureen, at a mission conference at Port-au-Prince. She continued her studies to graduate with a diploma in public health nursing. I am so proud of her."

André and Maureen had been married four years and were blessed with two children, a boy and a girl. André felt loved. His self-esteem enjoyed an all-time high.

André and Maureen reserved Monday evenings from six to nine as their "family night." They played games, listened to music, and prepared their meals together. Maureen called these particular suppers family fun times. They all pitched in from boiling water for tea to deciding a game to play. "We create our own entertainment." André said, lugging his two children, wrapped around his legs.

The cell phone jangled. The family expected a call from Henri, André's father, who was visiting friends in Les Cayes. "I'd better answer." André smiled. "Dad's right on time. He said he'd call about now," as he glanced at his watch. His kids untangled themselves from his legs and rolled on the floor laughing.

André picked up the phone. He said, "Hello, André Arnaud, Principal of Sunshine Academy speaking."

"I'm wrong. It's from New York." he shouted to Maureen.

"Hold on for a minute. It's hard for me to hear you." Holding his phone away from his mouth, he shouted, "You kids quiet down. I've got to hear." He picked up his phone, cupping his hand over his ear. "Sorry for the interruption. It's okay now."

The caller identified himself as a producer of "This is Haiti," a series for World Educational Television – New York. He then explained the purpose of his call.

After five minutes of listening, André said, "Yes, I understand. Welcome to Haiti. Please give me that arrival time and flight number again…Okay, I've got them and the names. Thanks!…I'll meet their plane Friday morning at the Camp Perrin airport." He clicked off, laying the phone on the hallway table.

Maureen served Haitian beans, rice with fish, and limeade. "What's that all about?" she asked.

"We're going to have two special guests Friday. A Rick Smith and Roger Dunlap are flying in to film Sunshine Academy. I'm to pick them up at Camp Perrin at 10:00 a.m. Friday."

"For whom?" Maureen asked.

"World Educational Television, New York," André answered.

"How long will they stay?" Maureen asked.

"Two days. Let's pray for a safe flight. This should be lots of fun and great publicity for the school!" André smiled.

Friday morning the clouds churned into greyish rolls over Macaya. Their light aircraft glided to a bouncing stop at Camp Perrin.

The pilot retrieved all personal baggage while his two passengers hunched and unloaded their gear of tripods and camera equipment.

Accompanied by his pet dog, André welcomed them.

Rick Smith bent down to pet the dog. "What's his name?" he asked.

André laughed and smiled. "John Wesley the Third."

"That's an unusual name for a dog," Smith remarked.

"He's a Methodist," André laughed. "Has a son named Frances Asbury."

"For a big litter you've always got Jesus's twelve disciples," quipped Roger Dunlap.

"Minus Judas," Rick Smith added.

"I can tell you guys and I are going to get along fine." André's smile broadened.

"Hop in the back of 'Sweet Chariot', our school's official taxi." The Jeep's name adorned the door of the four-wheel drive above the words 'Sunshine Academy, Mount Macaya.'

"We've got an hour's drive to get to the school," André said.

"Good!" said Dunlap. "I want to shoot some footage of the local environment as we travel. It'll set the stage and provide some background for our interviews."

On a hairpin turn, Dunlap almost lost his grip on his camera as the jeep whined and jerked. John Wesley the Third's tongue dripped and his tail wagged nervously from all the excitement.

Next morning, after a breakfast of Maureen's Haitian spaghetti, Smith and Dunlap toured the school, then were ushered into André's office.

"Light's perfect! Great for filming!" Dunlap observed.

The interview went smoothly. Students and faculty came and went, each telling about their own backgrounds and what brought them to Sunshine Academy.

Maureen's stories were particularly touching.

She revealed she was raised by her mother, a seamstress in Jacmel. Her father had left Haiti to live in Miami when she was six. For a while he had sent money home for her education. Then stopped. She looked down. "I never saw him again. He drifted out of our lives. And then," she continued, "Christ entered my life. My life changed at a mission clinic." She proudly raised her stethoscope and laughed.

Rick Smith nodded to André. "And now it's your turn. I'll ask the questions."

After an hour of reviewing André's background and work, Smith asked, "Why did you choose to remain in Haiti? You're in the midst of poverty and so little hope. Why?"

André smiled. "Poverty, yes. Despair sometimes. No hope. Never! My faith strengthens me. It's the power of Jesus' love and the spirit of Christ in my life that keep me going."

He looked squarely at Rick. "Please remember, God gave me the opportunity to briefly experience what many of these children live all their lives. Disrespect. Humiliation. Filth. Starvation. Beatings…and many children also have to endure sexual assault. I could go on and on…" André's voice trailed off into a whisper.

He sipped some water and continued. "I now understand their fears. Their innermost feelings of total abandonment. We, here at Sunshine, are their hope – Maureen, our faculty and all those who support us."

Emotionally shaken, Smith continued the interview. "Do you feel, André, that there will be an end coming to all this child slavery?"

André reached out for Maureen's hand. She stood behind him. "The end to all this will come when the majority of our world acts to stop this madness, this tragic nightmare – this destruction of innocent children. We must replace this sin of ignoring them with Christian compassion and proper education."

His voice faded. "My belief is that it will take generations. The hope of our world is children now and those of future generations."

André looked at the ceiling. His voice trembled. Maureen handed a handkerchief to wipe away his tears. "Sorry. I get so emotional," he said, drinking a cup of water.

Smith gazed tearfully around the room. "We'll leave it there for now." He walked across the room, followed by Dunlap. They hugged André and Maureen.

Smith added concluding remarks to their filming session. "In Haiti they have a saying in Creole: "*Kont li nou féb, men ansanm nou fo*" ("Alone we are weak, but together we are strong"). That's the reason Roger and I are here. People, young and old, wherever you are, Christ needs you. 'Help us now!' cry the children in slavery in Haiti."

"God bless you," André replied. He reached out and patted both men on their shoulders.

Is Haiti condemned to poverty forever?

Not at all. The most hopeful thing about Haiti is the refusal of its poor to give up and resign themselves to perpetual poverty, corruption and illiteracy.

Advances are being made in job training. Reforestation is underway in massive plantings. Agricultural, medical and business development are launched each year to meet the needs of all. As these efforts reach more people, hope continues to grow.

Christian churches and schools are experiencing growth. A new caring leadership is appearing. Gradually, if this continues, there will be far less poverty and a revitalized healthy nation will emerge.

25

The Unexpected Guest

A week passed. Dunlap and Smith emailed and phoned their gratitude for the gracious hospitality they received at Sunshine Academy. World Educational Television would air their interview in two weeks.

André surveyed Sunshine's school campus from his office window. The morning air steamed.

He watched two of his workmen running toward him. They carried a young teen, his arms flopping. He rushed to meet them outside. "We found him unconscious at the front gate, Dr. André. Your dog was licking his face."

"Lay him out flat on my desk. I'll get a stretcher from the storage room." André said. "We'll take him to the school clinic. He may have serious injuries."

He phoned Maureen, his wife, to meet them at the school clinic. "It's an emergency, Maureen. Have your triage staff ready. We're coming as quickly as we can."

The workmen shuffled and carried their stretcher bearing the injured youth into the exam room.

Sunshine's emergency staff were graduates preparing for nursing careers. They lifted the young stranger onto the examination bed.

The boy opened his eyes. Too weak to sit, he looked at André. Dried blood on his cheeks. His clothes were filthy and ripped.

He whispered, "You are Monsieur André."

"Yes."

The boy rolled his head to one side and said, "At last I've found you."

"What's your name?" Maureen asked.

"J-J-J-Jean," he coughed.

Maureen said, "Jean is a wonderful name. Same as my brother."

Maureen took his pulse. She listened to his heart and checked him for bleeding. "I see no signs of internal injuries," Maureen said. She carefully moved his arms and legs. "Bruised, but no broken bones."

"He's suffering from severe malnutrition and heat exhaustion. Let's cool him down with cold compresses. He must drink lots of water. We'll feed him soft foods later, as he recovers."

"Th-Th-Thank you!" he stuttered. He opened

his eyes and blinked.

"For now, please rest." Maureen softly swabbed the caked blood from the lad's face. She placed a cool, damp cloth on the boy's forehead.

They cut his ragged clothes off and gave him a warm sponge bath, then dressed him in a clean hospital gown.

"We'll never leave you. Someone will be here all the time. For now you need to sleep. We love you, child." Maureen softly soothed Jean's forehead with a cool wet cloth.

The hospital staff gathered around his battered body and prayed for his recovery.

Shortly after midnight, the boy awakened and asked for food. A nurse lifted his head. His swollen lips parted to swallow a few tablespoons of soft corn meal gruel. He lay back in a deep sleep all through the night.

The early morning sun beamed into the clinic's recovery room.

Jean awoke from a nightmare. Believing that Madam Noir was beating him, he raised his bandaged arms to deflect her blows.

"You're all right here, my dear. You're in the mission hospital," the nurse said. "Just rest quietly. If you hurt somewhere, please let me know," the nurse said.

The boy mumbled "André. André. André."

"I'll get him for you." She called the Arnaud home. "Dr. André, the boy's asking for you. Please come now."

At the Sunshine mission hospital, André held Jean's hand. "I'm here, Jean. I'm André. You asked for me."

"Thank you for saving me," Jean replied.

"Where are you from?" André asked.

"I was a restavec at Madame Noir's in Port-au-Prince. I escaped a week ago."

"But why here, Jean?" André smoothed Jean's hair.

"For years I heard Madame Noir mention how you escaped the day her husband died."

"Yes, I remember his death mentioned on T.V. But I don't remember when or how."

Jean weakly nodded. "The morning you and the hutia left. A heart attack."

"So you know about the hutia?"

"Yes, is it still alive?"

"No, he died a few years ago of old age. Hoot became our school mascot," André said. "We'll talk later. You must rest. Do you need the bathroom?"

Jean rolled his head "no" and then lapsed into sleep.

Late that afternoon, Jean wanted to talk. André

brought him some ice cream.

André leaned closer. "Did you know Jabou, Madame Noir's brother?"

"Know him! He's my father!"

"Your father!" André's jaw dropped in disbelief. "And your mother?"

"Beatrice, Madame Noir's daughter. I am their love child."

"How were you treated?"

Jean froze, as if he had been severely tortured.

"Here, finish your ice cream first. I'll be back in a little while." André noticed that Jean's face was drained of all emotion. The dish of ice cream slipped from Jean's hands and fell to the floor.

An hour passed. André returned. "You look awake, Jean. Have a little cat nap?"

Jean nodded 'yes' and smiled.

"As I was asking you earlier, how did Jabou and your mother treat you?"

"I never saw Jabou again. He fled to the Dominican Republic. Madame hired two thugs to kill him."

"Did they?"

"I never knew."

"And Beatrice, your mother?"

"She loved me. She and the cook treated me like a son. I was her baby until I was ten."

"Ten?"

"Yes."

"What happened?"

"She was killed in a car wreck. Ran her sports car off a cliff into the ocean. She drowned. Then things changed."

"How so?"

"Madame Noir forced me to live chained at night. Called me a restavec. An animal. She hated me, and beat me often.

"I worked as her personal slave. She cursed me. Told me I should have been murdered or aborted."

Jean coughed and cleared his throat.

"I endured her beatings and starvation for three years. I stole food to survive. Last week I drugged her rum with sleeping pills. The cook's daughter helped me escape and here I am."

Exhausted, Jean propped himself back on his pillow.

André asked, "Do you know what happened to Madame Noir?"

"No, Monsieur André. Do you?"

André answered. "The Port-au-Prince TV news channel announced yesterday she died from liver failure. She left one survivor, her son Michael, who has immigrated to France and works for a casino in Monte Carlo. Madame Noir is totally out of our lives now, Jean."

"Tomorrow is a new day for you Jean. Welcome to Sunshine Academy. As soon as you are healed and well, it's back to school and 'futbol'." Maureen and André held hands with Jean, prayed with him, then hugged and kissed him. "Good night, Jean. We love you." John Wesley the Third, the family dog, climbed on the bed and licked Jean's hand.

André and Maureen turned out the lights and tiptoed into the hallway.

"I can hardly wait for Jean to tell us how he found us and Sunshine," Maureen whispered.

"I'll bet it's an exciting story!" André remarked, half smiling, pensively pursing his lips.

"Look who's talking?" Maureen laughed.

Prevent a Child from Becoming Enslaved!

Act Immediately!

1. **Work** with others in your youth group or family to sponsor an orphan or impoverished child to attend school, which will greatly diminish the chance that the child will become a restavec. Hope for Haiti's Children's child sponsorship program is unique in Haiti since 100% of the funds donated each month are used in the sponsorship (0% for fund-raising and general administration). For more information or to sponsor a child, go to www.HopeForHaitisChildren.org.

2. **Invite** missionaries from Haiti and Haitians living near you to speak to your class.

3. **Consult** your local school, church and public librarians for further reading lists, DVD's and film resources, websites, and organizations dedicated to ending child slavery

4. **Pray** for restavec children in slavery!

Haiti Activities
for School and Church

■ Encourage your family, small group, class, school, youth group, or entire church to organize an Orphan Care Sunday.

www.OrphanCareSunday.org

The participants learn and pray about the needs of orphaned children in Haiti, eat a simple Haitian meal together, and donate what they would have spent in a restaurant to help Christian orphanages in Haiti.

■ Eat a meal of beans and rice. Discuss how Haitian orphans live. Support an orphanage.

■ Write and perform a one-act play. Imagine you are a slave. Discuss how child slavery can be abolished.

■ Sponsor a program of Haitian music and instruments.

■ Construct a model of a Haitian village.

■ Raise money to dig a village well in Haiti.

■ Plant a Haitian vegetable garden at your school. Discuss life in rural Haiti.

Be creative. You are only limited by your desire for knowledge and imagination.

Escape to Macaya

Suggested Reading List for Beginning Study

Anderson, Mildred. Illustrator: Cole, Anita. *Beyond All This: Thirty Years with the Mountain People of Haiti.* Grand Rapids: Baptist Haiti Mission, 1979. Print. 216 pages. ISBN 9781611530360.

Cadet, Jean-Robert. *My Stone of Hope: From Haitian Slave Child to Abolitionist.* United States of America: University of Texas Press, 2011. Print. 224 pages. ISBN 978-0-292-72853.

Dash, J. Michael. *Culture and Customs of Haiti.* Culture and Customs of Latin America, Series Editor Peter Standish. Glenwood Press, Wesport, Conneticut. 2011. Print. 200 pages. ISBN 978-0313360992.

Kidder, Tracy. *Mountains Beyond Mountains: The Quest of Dr. Paul Farmer, A Man Who Would Cure the World.* United States of America: Random House, 2004. 317 pages. ISBN 0-375-50616-0.

Pierre, Rev. Dr. Jacques E. *Haiti: Challenges and Hopes*, with Study Leader's Guide. United Methodist Church, Women's Division, General Board of Global Ministries, 2011. Print. 122 pages. ISBN 978-1-933663-51-7. Library of Congress Control Number: 2010939380.

Temple, Frances. *Taste of Salt: A Story of Modern Haiti.* New York: Orchard Books, 1992. Print. 192 pages. ISBN 0-531-05459-4.

Escape to Macaya

Additional Bibliography

Aristide, Jean-Bertrand. *Eyes of the Heart: Seeking A Path for the Poor in the Age of Globalization.* Ed. Laura Flynn. Common Courage Press, Monroe, ME. 2000. Print. 112 pages. ISBN 978-1567511871.

Clammer, Paul, Michael Grosberg, and Kevin Raub. *Dominican Republic and Haiti.* Lonely Planet Publications Pty Ltd. Oakland, CA. 2008. Print. 368 pages. ISBN 978-1741794564.

Danticat, Edwidge. *After the Dance: A Walk Through Carnival in Jacmel,* Haiti. New York: Crown Publishers, 2002. Print. 158 pages. ISBN 0-609-60908-4.

Danticat, Edwidge. *Behind the Mountains.* New York: Scholastic Inc. Orchard Books. 2002. Print. 166 pages. ISBN 0-439-37299-2.

Desmangles, Leslie. *The Faces of the Gods.* Chapel Hill & London: The University of North Carolina Press, 1992. Print. 218 pages. ISBN 0-8078-2059-8 (hardback); ISBN 0-8078-4393-8 (paperback).

Girard, Philippe. *Haiti: The Tumultous History - From Pearl of the Caribbean to Broken Nation.* Palgrave/Macmillan. 2010. Print. 256 pages. ISBN 978-0230106611.

Gold, Herbert. *Best Nightmare on Earth: A Life in Haiti.* New York: Prentice Hall Press, 1991. Print. 303 pages. ISBN 0-13-372327-5.

Griffiths, Leslie. *History of Methodism in Haiti.* Port-au-Prince, 1991. Print. ASIN: B0014S5MI2.

Halverson , Delia. *Krik, Krak: The Story of Haiti.* Children's Mission Study and Teacher's Guide. Women's Division, The General Board of Global Ministries, The United Methodist Church, 2011.

Loederer, Richard. *Voodoo Fire.* Garden City: The Country Life Press, 1935. Print. 274 pages. ISBN-10: 1589803620. ISBN-13: 978-1589803626.

Mystic Fire Video. *Divine Horsemen: The Living Gods of Haiti.* Dir. Maya Deren. Mystic Fire Video, 1985. Video. Filmed 1947-1951.

Pierre-Okerson, Judith; Paul Jeffrey, and Sema Samuel. *Haiti: Perspectives on a Living History: Inspiring Stories of Beauty, Strength, and Courage.* United Methodist Women. www.unitedmethodistwomen.org (video).

Skinner, Benjamin E. *A Crime So Monstrous: Face-to-face with Modern-Day Slavery.* Free Press, New York, 2008. Print. 328 pages. ISBN 978-0-7432-9007-4.

Straub, Gerard Thomas. *Hidden In The Rubble: A Haitian Pilgrimage of Compassion and Resurrection.* Orbis Books, Maryknoll, NY. 2010. Print. 192 pages. ISBN 978-1570758973.

Taft, Edna. *A Puritan in Voodoo-Land.* Philadelphia: The Penn Publishing Company, 1938. Print. 407 pages.

US Department of State. *Trafficking in Persons Report.* June 2012. Web. 10 June 2013.
http://www.state.gov/documents/organization/192587.pdf

Weddle, Ken. *Haiti in Pictures* (Visual Geography Series). Minneapolis: Lerner Publications Company, 1987. Print. 64 Pages. ISBN 0-8225-1816-3.

Wilentz, Amy. *The Rainy Season Haiti - Then and Now.* Simon and Schuster, Inc., New York, N.Y., 1989. Print. 448 pages. ISBN 978-1439198391.

Williams, Karen Lynn. *Tap-Tap.* New York: Clarion Books, 1994. Print. 34 pages. ISBN 0-395-65617-6.

Wolkstein, Diane. *The Magic Orange Tree: and Other Haitian Folktales.* New York: Schocken Books, 1997. Print. 224 pages. ISBN 0-8052-0650-7.

Wydick, Bruce. *Want to Change the World? Sponsor a Child.* Christianity Today, June 2013.
www.christianitytoday.com/ct/2013/june/want-to-change-world-sponsor-a-child.html

Escape to Macaya

Research Resources

- Consult your school and church librarians for further reading lists, DVD's and film resources, websites, and organizations dedicated to ending child slavery.

- Interview your church leaders and missions committee for specific information about your church's involvment with Haiti (e.g. study programs and projects to help Haiti's children).

- Invite missionaries and Haitians to speak to your class.

Organizations to Contact for More Information

Hope for Haiti's Children (Church of Christ)
P.O. Box 62328
Cincinnati, OH 45262-0328

www.HopeForHaitisChildren.org
- Child Sponsorship
- Orphan Care Sponsorship
- Daily Bread Sponsorship
- Christmas Joy Boxes
- Medical Mission Trips
- Volunteer Opportunities
- Orphan Care Sunday Materials
  www.OrphanCareSunday.org

United Methodist Missions in Haiti

http://new.gbgm-umc.org/umcor/work/emergencies/ongoing/haitiearthquake/

http://www.umvimhaiti.org/

Volunteers
http://new.gbgm-umc.org/about/us/mv/haiti/resources/

Relief Resources UMCOR
http://new.gbgm-umc.org/umw/haiti/resources/

Methodist Guest House
The Methodist Guest House is located in Petionville, a suburb of Port-au-Prince. It is owned and operated by the Methodist Church of Haiti. It provides meals and overnight stay for short term missionaries. Contact can be made through
http://www.umvimhaiti.org.

Other Books by
Dr. Hall Duncan, "Dr. D"

Dr. Duncan is the author of numerous books for young people and seniors.

Visit his website for information about these and other books for the whole family.

www.hallduncan.com

172

Order Additional Copies of *Escape to Macaya*

CUSTOMER INFORMATION

NAME: _____

COMPANY: _____

ADDRESS: _____

CITY: _____

STATE: _____ ZIP: _____ PHONE: _____

PROVINCE _____ COUNTRY: _____

EMAIL: _____

All orders must be prepaid.
Paperback edition and digital format are available online at www.amazon.com.

PAYMENT INFORMATION

CARD NO: ☐☐☐☐☐☐☐☐☐☐☐☐☐☐☐☐

EXP. DATE: ☐☐ / ☐☐

Make check or money order payable in U.S.
dollars to HUMOR & COMMUNICATION LLC

○ VISA
○ MasterCard
○ Check
○ Money Order

SIGNATURE: _____

ORDER FORM

Title	Quantity	Price Each	TOTAL
Escape to Macaya Paperback		$ 11.99	
*Standard Shipping & Handling Charges Within the Continental United States 1 – 3 Books - $7.50 4 Books or more – Call or email for details		Add Your State or Local Tax	$
*Standard Shipping Rates for Alaska, Hawaii & Puerto Rico 1 – 3 Books - $9.50 4 Books or more – Call or email for details Please allow 14 – 21 days for shipping after receipt of your book order.		Shipping & Handling (See Table at left)	$
		TOTAL	
Other countries, request quotation		**PREPAYMENT REQUIRED** Discounts Available for orders with more than 25 copies. Request quote. **orders@hallduncan.com** *Shipping rates are subject to change without notice.	

Send Orders to: Humor & Communication LLC
                  P.O. Box 7104
                  Edmond, OK 73083

Made in the USA
Charleston, SC
26 July 2014